THE
KEEPER
OF THE
CASTLE

THE-LOU

ASPIRE
PUBLISHING HUB LLC.

The Keeper of the Castle
Copyright © 2024 by THE-LOU

All rights reserved. No part of this publication may be reproduced, distributed, or transmitted in any form or by any means, including photocopying, recording, or other electronic or mechanical methods, without the prior written permission of the author, except in the case of brief quotations embodied in critical reviews and certain other non-commercial uses permitted by copyright law.

ISBN
978-1-962611-67-1 (Paperback)
978-1-962611-68-8 (eBook)

Table of Contents

Chapter I 1

Chapter II 4

Chapter III 15

Chapter IV 24

Chapter V 30

Chapter VI 34

Chapter VII 39

Chapter VIII 45

Chapter IX 57

Chapter X 66

Chapter XI 77

Chapter XII 84

Chapter XIII 92

Chapter XIV 101

Chapter XV 115

Chapter XVI 122

Chapter XVII 131

Chapter XVIII 137

Chapter XIX 144

Chapter XX 176

Inside the hallway, the air is filled with the chaotic noise of men screaming and hollering profanities. The sound of cell doors opening and closing rings out loudly. As the footsteps grow louder, five men walk together, four dressed in guards' uniforms and one in a suit. Their backs are turned as one of the guards unlocks a massive metal door, revealing a large group of unruly men inside. The prisoners are acting uncivilized, yelling, screaming, and even engaging in fights. The guards within the room attempt to break up the commotion.

Moving inside the auditorium, the four guards and the man in the suit walk toward the stage, still facing away from the camera. The prisoners notice their presence and begin yelling obscenities, directing their insults, particularly toward the man in the suit.

"Hey, everybody! Look who's here? Our new BITCH warden=. HA! HA!" Prisoner 1 exclaims, drawing attention to the arrival of the new warden.

On the warden's first day at the prison, an unexpected incident unfolded as he walked through the crowd of inmates. A mocking voice rang out, "Fuck you warden! Punk ass motherfucker! HA! HA!" Instantly, a ripple of laughter spread among the prisoners, much to the warden's surprise and dismay. Caught off guard, he felt a mix of puzzlement and sadness.

Raising his arms fully extended, the warden pleads, "Would everyone please be quiet?"

While some prisoners begin to calm down, the majority continue their unruly behavior.

"What the hell are you getting ready to do? Split the Red Sea? HA! HA!" Prisoner 2 jeers sarcastically.

"No! He is going to make it rain. HA! HA!" adds Prisoner 3, joining in the mockery.

Angrily, the warden's expression transformed and she yelled, "I want everybody to sit down and shut up! Please!" the warden commands, his frustration evident in his tone.

Gradually, the prisoners quiet down, and the guards assist in making the remaining prisoners sit in their seats.

"Thank you! I'm the new warden at the Missouri State Department of Corrections, as some of you already know. My name is John Blake, but all my friends call me Jack," the warden introduces himself, attempting to establish rapport. He smiles and continues, "Hopefully, we can all become friends and get along with one another. What do you say?"

Interrupting Jack, Prisoner 1 interjects, "Nobody here wants to be your friend, Jack. (Pauses) ASS!"

Laughter resounds once again among the prisoners, and Jack's anger resurfaces.

"Look here! I've only been here two weeks, and all I've faced is constant name-calling. I will not tolerate this kind of abuse. I called everyone here to formally introduce myself and let you all know that everyone deserves a second chance. I am already in hot water because of my belief in rehabilitation. It could potentially jeopardize my chances of becoming the governor of Missouri, but I am unwavering in my convictions. I will fight for what I believe in, whether you like it or not! I am determined to prove that hardened criminals can be rehabilitated and reintegrated into society's best. If you refuse to work with me, I won't continue to bend over backwards for you!" Jack passionately expresses his determination, his frustration evident in his voice.

"You all heard the warden!" exclaimed Jack with a mischievous grin. "He wants to be your friend. So if that is true, instead of bending over backward, he should bend over forward. Just like he said, 'we could all get along just fine.' HA! HA!" Deliverance said.

All of the prisoners burst into laughter, exchanging high fives. Jack rested his face on the stand he was speaking from and shook his head back and forth.

The guard, David, stood on stage with Jack and conversed with his fellow guard, Jerry, who stood beside him.

"I don't know why he put up with this shit," David commented.

"I know what you mean. If it were me, I would put that motherfucker in the hole right now," Jerry responded.

Unbeknownst to the guards, Jack overheard their conversation. He lifted his head and walked over to them.

"Jerry, you are my lieutenant and David, you are my captain," Jack addressed them sternly. "Now, if you guys have the same evil minds as the prisoners, tell me, how are we going to rehabilitate these guys? Now, as long as I am the warden here, I don't want to hear anything that is negative. Do you two understand?"

"Yes, Sir!" David and Jerry responded in unison.

"OK," Jack acknowledged, satisfied with their response.

Jack returned to the stand, positioning himself in front of the microphone.

"Now, I am going to forget everything I have heard up until this point, but I am asking you all to please give me a chance to help," Jack pleaded. "Just think of what I can do if I am elected Governor. There could be better living conditions for everyone, plus better food and anything else you all can think of that you want. I need your support in here, just as much as I need it on the outside. So, what do you all say?"

Jack wore a broad smile, but the prisoners responded with solemn frowns. No one uttered a word.

"Well, I know you all don't believe me," Jack continued, undeterred by their lack of response, "but I have a surprise for some of you, and who knows, if we can work things out, maybe any of you could be next."

"What does he have for us? Weekend passes?" Prisoner 2 snickered.

"If that's what it is, I hope he calls my name," Prisoner 3 added optimistically.

"When I call your name, please stand up," Jack announced, motioning for one of the guards to bring him the list. He glanced at the list, a look of confusion crossing his face.

"I thought there were supposed to be more names on here," Jack murmured.

"Sorry, Sir, this is all that they would do," the guard apologized.

"OK, well, it's better than nothing. Thank you," Jack acknowledged, trying to hide his disappointment.

Jack cleared his throat and addressed the prisoners once again.

"Lincoln Jones, please stand up," Jack said with a smile.

"Don't call me that! The name is K-9," Lincoln snapped.

Jack looked at him incredulously, taken aback by the response.

"OK, if that is what you prefer, K-9," Jack acquiesced. He continued, "Would Francis Johnson please stand up?"

Some of the prisoners burst into laughter.

"Don't call me that! The name is Da-Bo," Francis asserted.

Jack glanced at him with a bemused expression.

"Whispering to the guard," Jack asked, "Where in the hell do they come up with these names? I guess I can't blame Francis, having a name like that in a place like this. But you would think he would come up with a better name than Da-Bo."

The guard shrugged his shoulders, appearing just as clueless.

"Well, you two guys and your fellow inmates will be happy to hear that you are going to be set free one week from today," Jack announced.

Jack began to applaud, but the prisoners responded with boos and erratic behavior. K-9 and Da-Bo seemed angrier than the other prisoners. Jack couldn't comprehend their reaction.

"What's wrong? Aren't you guys happy for them?" Jack inquired, perplexed.

"Hell naw!" Prisoner 1 shouted, and the rest of the prisoners joined in, expressing their disapproval.

Jack addressed K-9 and Da-Bo, a hint of confusion in his voice. "Maybe I can understand why these guys are mad, but I can't understand why you two are mad."

K-9 leaned forward, his expression serious. "Man, some of these dudes in here have life, and some are on death row. They don't give a fuck! If they find out someone is getting out, they will do anything to fuck it up, even kill you if it came down to it."

Da-Bo nodded in agreement. "That is right. You never tell anyone how much time you have in prison. Now that they know we are getting out, anything could happen to us."

Meanwhile, the guards stood in the background, shaking their heads. David whispered to Jerry, "He's got a lot to learn."

Jerry sighed, his voice filled with concern. "This is going to be rough. I hope I can last."

Jack turned to the guard, his voice barely a whisper. "Is what they're saying true?"

The guard nodded solemnly. "I'm afraid so, Sir."

Jack shook his head, struggling to grasp the harsh reality. "Guards, please bring these two men up here with me."

The guards complied with Jack's request, escorting K-9 and Da-Bo closer to him.

"I will hide you men out so nothing will happen to you. Deal?" Jack offered, a glimmer of hope in his eyes.

K-9 and Da-Bo exchanged glances before nodding in agreement. "Fine with us."

Jack turned to David. "David, please take these men to my office. No one will bother them there."

"Yes, Sir," David acknowledged, leading the two prisoners away from the crowd.

"Now, please don't be mad. Look on the bright side; it could be any one of you next," Jack tried to reassure the rest of the prisoners.

However, the prisoners responded with renewed boos and protests as Jack and the guards made their exit from the stage.

Suddenly, a voice broke through the commotion. "Hey warden! Hey warden!"

A prisoner struggled against the restraints of two guards, catching Jack's attention. Jack approached him, a curious expression on his face.

"Yes, Sir, and what can I do for you?" Jack asked, willing to listen.

The prisoner's frustration was evident in his voice. "I have been in this motherfucker for 15 years. How come they get to go free and I don't? Those two punks haven't even done a year yet!"

Jack took a moment to consider the prisoner's words. "Well, their names came up on the computer."

"Fuck the computer! This is not the lottery. This is life, and I am doing it. You understand?" the prisoner retorted, his anger unabated.

Jack offered a glimmer of hope. "Well, I will do my best to look into it."

The prisoner, clearly dissatisfied with Jack's response, continued to be restrained by the guards. Jack and the guards left the auditorium, leaving the crowd of prisoners in a state of discontent.

THE-LOU

In the dimly lit hallway, Jack and Jerry strolled side by side, their footsteps echoing softly against the cold, stone walls. Engrossed in conversation, they were discussing a particular prisoner who had been causing quite a stir within the prison walls.

"What is that prisoner's name?" Jack asked, his curiosity piqued.

"Oliver Mitchell, but of course, he doesn't want to be called that," Jerry replied.

"Oh yeah! So what does he want to be called?" Jack inquired further.

"Mutt Dog!" Jerry answered, causing Jack to stop walking and burst into laughter.

"Where in the hell do they get these names from?" Jack wondered aloud, amused by the peculiar moniker.

They continued down the hall, their backs to the camera, engrossed in conversation.

In Jack Blake's kitchen, LaDonna, his wife, bustled around preparing dinner. Jack, along with their two children, Jack Jr. and Linda, eagerly anticipated the delicious meal she was cooking.

"Mom, when are we going to eat? I'm starving," Jack Jr. exclaimed.

"Yeah! Me too," Linda chimed in.

"Don't rush your mother; she is doing the best she can. Some people need help with microwave dinners. HA! HA!" Jack teased, trying to lighten the mood.

"I'm going to throw your ass in this microwave if you don't shut up," LaDonna jokingly threatened.

"Please, don't use that kind of language. I hear enough of that at work," Jack gently reprimanded her.

Curious about his new job, LaDonna turned to Jack, still busy preparing dinner. "So how do you like your new job? You've been there a couple of weeks, but you don't talk too much about it."

"I'm still getting a feel for it, but I must admit, I was initiated today," Jack shared.

Pausing to put dinner on the table, LaDonna inquired, "What do you mean by that?"

"Well, I called a meeting to introduce myself. At first, they started calling me a bunch of names I don't care to repeat—they would not give me any respect. They acted like a pack of wild animals," Jack explained, a tinge of frustration in his voice.

Laughing softly, LaDonna responded, "Well honey, some of those men have been locked up for a long time, and they would be a little resentful."

"Resentful is not the word to describe them. They were downright ignorant. And I just can't get over those names they gave themselves," Jack continued, his disbelief evident.

Curious, Linda interjected, "K-9. Like a dog, Daddy?"

"That's right, baby, and that is just how they acted," Jack confirmed, his tone filled with astonishment.

"Well, it sounds like you've got your hands full. Do you still think they can be rehabilitated?" LaDonna questioned, concerned.

"Well, I'm going to give it a shot," Jack replied, determined.

LaDonna expressed her thoughts, "You know, that may be the one thing that will keep you from becoming Governor, plus you're a black man."

"I know what you mean, but think about this. The mayor of St. Louis is black, and so is the mayor of Kansas City. I have their support, and everyone is supporting them. Wouldn't it be strange if the only way I was going to become Governor was because I'm black? I know for a fact that they do not agree with me on some of my issues. Well, hell, most of them are behind me because I am black," Jack shared, contemplating the complexities of politics.

LaDonna chuckled, "Yeah! Whoever would have thought that being black would work to your advantage!"

"Let's say the blessing and eat. I want to get a little rest before I go to this press conference," Jack suggested, shifting the conversation to the present.

Surprised by the mention of a press conference, LaDonna commented, "I didn't know you had a press conference today."

"It's really no big deal. It will only last about fifteen or twenty minutes. The guy running against me, Missouri State Senator John Beck, may be there too. So I need to be on time or a little early to get the upper hand," Jack explained, strategizing for the event.

"As far as I am concerned, you will always have the upper hand," LaDonna assured him.

"Of course, you know us Harvard men always get what we want, and to prove it, I have the most beautiful woman in the world," Jack expressed his affection.

"And I have the greatest man in the world," LaDonna reciprocated, their display of affection interrupted by their children's frowns.

"Don't do that in front of us," Linda protested.

"Yeah! Because you two are going to get carried away, and I will have another little sister I don't want," Jack Jr. added, causing Jack and LaDonna to be taken aback.

"Now, what does an eight-year-old know about that?" Jack questioned, trying to make sense of his son's remark.

"Well, I know that the stork didn't bring us here," Jack Jr. replied, matter-of-factly.

"Daddy! Daddy! I know," Linda chimed in. "You see, the man sticks his thing inside the woman, and then we come out."

Shocked by their children's knowledge, Jack exclaimed, "Who's been telling you two about all of these things?"

"Lathisha," Linda replied innocently.

Looking at LaDonna, Jack voiced his concern, "You see! I told you that your sister's kids were going to be a bad influence on them."

"What are you trying to say, Daddy? It's not true?" Jack Jr. asked, seeking clarification.

"Well, they were going to find out sooner or later, so don't be blaming my sister's kids," LaDonna defended, normalizing the conversation.

"I was hoping it would be later than sooner. I don't agree with an eight or six-year-old knowing about sex like this," Jack confessed, his parental instincts kicking in.

"Well, it's the real world. Face it," LaDonna concluded, accepting the reality of their children's exposure to certain topics.

"Enough of this. Let's say the blessing and eat," Jack redirected the conversation, seeking to regain a sense of normalcy in their family mealtime.

In Jack's bedroom, he jolted awake, realizing it was already six o'clock. Frustrated, he swiftly leaped out of bed.

"Damn! Damn! Damn! LaDonna, I told you to wake me up at five fifteen. Now I'm going to be late!" Jack exclaims, his annoyance evident.

LaDonna rushes into the bedroom, concerned. "Do you need any help? I am sorry I let you oversleep."

"Just pick me out something to wear while I'm in the bathroom," Jack instructs, rushing to get ready.

Outside Jack's House- Big house with a large front yard:

The garage door opens, and Jack pulls out in his Cadillac.

Outside the Hotel- Where the press conference is being held:

Jack arrives and the valet parks his car. As soon as he steps out, reporters flock to greet him, but Jack is in a hurry and ignores their attempts to engage him.

Inside the Hotel- Lobby:

Jack is met by his friend Carl Davis, a prosecuting attorney.

"Jack, where have you been? You're late. I've been waiting down here for you. Come on and follow me, and I'll show you where to go," Carl says, slightly annoyed.

"When did it start?" Jack asks, realizing the lateness of his arrival.

"About fifteen minutes ago. I wish you could've been on time because Senator John Beck is eating you alive. Why didn't you tell me that you pardoned two cons that hadn't even served a year in jail for robbery and aggravated assault?" Carl confronts him, disappointment was evident in his voice.

"I was. I just haven't gotten around to it," Jack admits, a hint of regret in his tone.

"Well, I want you to know that the Mayor Al Hopgood of St. Louis and Mayor Ervin of Kansas City are not happy about that decision, not to mention our own Mayor of Jefferson City, Mike Lomax, is quoted as saying that he is almost sorry he hired you for the position," Carl informs him, concerned about the repercussions.

"If they do not like what I'm doing, they can vote me out of my position. I'm going to do what I think is right, no matter what!" Jack asserts, determined to stand by his decisions.

"Can't you see that decisions like this just might cost you the election? Senator John Beck is jumping all over this one. So I want you to know what you're up against when we walk through these doors," Carl warns him, hoping Jack understands the gravity of the situation.

Outside the Ballroom:

Jack and Carl stand in front of the big double doors. Carl opens the door, and they enter the ballroom. Senator John Beck is still talking to the press on stage. Jack makes his way up on stage and takes his seat, catching John's attention.

"Well, isn't it nice to see that our warden has finally made it? Although it's none of my business, why are you late? You didn't have to make hotel reservations for those two criminals you set free in our society today, did you? HA! HA!" John taunts, drawing laughter from the crowd.

Whispering to Jack, Carl advises, "When it's your chance to talk, please make it good. This guy is gaining a lot of support."

Jack nods, understanding the importance of making a strong impression.

John Beck continues, "I know this press conference is not supposed to last long, and I have some personal matters I need to take care of myself. I will leave you all with this in mind. If anyone commits a crime, they should do the time. It is not fair to law-abiding citizens. Think for one minute what it would be like to have this guy for Governor, and he is the warden. Hell, I may even become a criminal because no matter what crime I commit, I know that I'm not going to be punished but almost rewarded."

The crowd reacts, some murmuring in agreement.

John Beck further fuels the argument, "Warden Jack Blake is talking about remodeling the prisons, better clothing, and whatever else you can think of for a bunch of people that don't deserve it. Just think of what it's going to cost you, the taxpayer. Somebody has to pay for this, and it's going to be the honest people of the State of Missouri. Now, do any of you want to see your hard-earned tax dollars go for a cause like this? I don't think so. Come election time, in two weeks, if you don't vote for John Beck for Governor, you are going to see the crime rate go sky high and your tax dollars out the window. Thank you all, and good night."

John Beck exits the stage, followed by a group of reporters. Jack rises from his seat and takes his position behind the microphone, ready to respond to the accusations and present his perspective.

Inside the Hotel Lobby, the reporters surround Jack, eager to question him after the press conference.

"Mr. Blake, in your opinion, how much of what Senator Beck is saying is true?" Reporter 1 asks, seeking clarification.

"Senator Beck has a very clever way of twisting the truth. I strongly believe in rehabilitation because some of these people never had a chance in life," Jack responds confidently.

"I also believe that with proper training, these men and women in our prison systems could learn valuable trades, get a decent job, and help our economy. Once they know what it's like to make decent money, they will no longer be a threat to society. If we can spend millions of dollars on parks and animals, how come we can't take some of that money and spend it on re-educating people? History has proven that cruel and unusual punishment has not helped anyone. Instead, they adjust to the living conditions, and when set free, they are more dangerous now than they were when they first got locked up. I want to put an end to the repeat offender forever. With the plan that I have, you can see that a person who was a menace to society can become a great and well-respected person in the community." He continues.

Another reporter, Reporter 2, chimes in, "Warden Blake, we all know that your financial management history is great, and I've seen some of the plans you have drawn up for ways of creating jobs, and I must admit that I think it's pretty impressive. Even Senator John Beck agreed with some of your ideas when questioned about them. You could win this election hands down if you didn't believe in rehabilitation so strongly. I would like to know why you would let a bunch of prisoners, or to most people, the scum of the earth, keep you from maybe winning this election. Are they that important?"

Jack takes a moment to gather his thoughts before responding, "I know that everyone feels that I'm going to waste state money on these prisoners. In the long run, it's going to turn out to be just the opposite. I am aware of the fact that it costs $75,000 per cellblock per year, $25,000 per prisoner. We are spending millions of dollars on healthcare and drug rehabs that are not working. All I want to do is try something different because what we have been doing for the last fifty years has not worked. What makes anyone think that the same barbaric system is going to work in the future?"

The Master of Ceremonies interrupts, "Well, time is up everyone, and I'll see you all right back here in two weeks for the real debate between Senator John Beck and Warden Jack Blake. Thank you and good night."

Inside the Hotel Lobby:

As everyone exits the room and the hotel, Jack and Carl walk together.

"Well, how do you think I did?" Jack asks Carl, seeking his opinion.

"I think you did good, but he might have you by the balls. I wish you wouldn't have released those prisoners until after the election," Carl admits, concerned about the potential impact of Jack's decisions.

"It is only three weeks before the election," Jack responds, slightly defensive.

"No, stupid! I'm talking about not even telling anybody until the election was over. I'm afraid to say, but I think that move might cost you the election," Carl expresses his worry.

Outside the hotel, Carl and Jack stood side by side, patiently waiting for their cars at the valet.

"Do you want to follow me over to Bert's for a drink?" Carl suggests.

"No thanks. I have a hard day tomorrow, and I need all the rest I can get. Maybe next time," Jack declines, prioritizing his rest.

Their cars arrive simultaneously. They bid farewell to each other, get into their cars, and drive off.

Outside the prison, a prominent sign read "Missouri State Department of Corrections."

Inside Jack's office, two beds flanked his desk—one occupied by K-9 and the other by Da-Bo. While Jack diligently worked on paperwork, the two loyal companions began making noises, which started to grate on his nerves. Frustrated, Jack slammed down his pen, seeking some peace and quiet.

"How many times do I have to tell you two? I need a quiet atmosphere here, okay?" Jack reprimands them, emphasizing the need for a peaceful environment.

"Damn! This is going to be a long week," Da-Bo mutters, expressing his frustration.

"Well, do you want to go back into G.P.?" Jack asks, referring to the general population.

"Hell no!" Da-Bo quickly responds, not willing to return to the regular prison environment.

"All right then, shut up. I want you to know that there are 2,000 guys that would love to be in your shoes," Jack reminds them, highlighting the privilege they have.

The phone rings, interrupting their conversation. Jack answers the call.

"Hello, Jack Blake speaking," he says.

"Sir, there is a package here for you, and the mail carrier needs your signature," David, one of the guards, informs him.

"Okay, I'll be right down," Jack responds, acknowledging the delivery.

Jack leaves the office, and as soon as the door closes, K-9 and Da-Bo start rummaging through Jack's coat pockets. K-9 discovers Jack's wallet.

"Look at what I found," K-9 exclaims, showing Da-Bo the wallet.

"How much money is in there?" Da-Bo asks eagerly.

"Who cares? We couldn't take that if we wanted to. He would notice it missing, stupid. But we can take these credit cards. Hell, he's got about 25 or 30 of them! He wouldn't notice that too quickly," K-9 suggests, realizing the potential opportunity.

"Well, hurry up and put it in your pocket before he brings his punk ass back in here," Da-Bo urges K-9 to act quickly.

K-9 pockets the credit cards and notices Jack's driver's license. He pulls it out and shows it to Da-Bo.

"You lived in Jefferson City for about five years, didn't you?" K-9 asks Da-Bo.

"Sure did. Why?" Da-Bo replies, curious about K-9's train of thought.

"You know where this address is?" K-9 asks, pointing at Jack's driver's license.

"I have an idea," Da-Bo responds, starting to see where K-9 is heading.

"Good because when we get out, we're going to pay him a little visit to show him our appreciation," K-9 declares, revealing his plan.

IV

Outside of the prison, exactly one week later, the prison gates swung open, and Da-Bo and K-9 stepped out, free men at last.

"Now that we are free men, what are we going to do?" Da-Bo asks, uncertain about their next steps.

"We are going to rent us a car with this credit card, then buy us a gun and break into the warden's house. You do remember the address, don't you?" K-9 suggests, outlining their plan.

"Man, I was thinking maybe we should just get our asses on the bus and forget about this shit. I mean, after all, he did let us go free," Da-Bo hesitates, questioning their chosen path.

"Yeah, I know. You ain't got to tell me, but answer this: How much money did they give you when you left that motherfucker?" K-9 challenges Da-Bo.

"$50.00," Da-Bo responds, realizing the insufficiency of their funds.

"Now, how long do you think that is gonna last?" K-9 asks, emphasizing the financial challenges they face.

"Not long," Da-Bo admits, realizing the urgency of their situation.

"All right then, we need some money, and ain't nobody gonna give us a job coming straight out of the pen. This is the perfect setup. We know whose house we're gonna rob, and we know he is not gonna be there," K-9 convinces Da-Bo of the plan's necessity.

"Okay, that sounds good, but when we go to use that card, everyone in this town knows him. How are we gonna get away with that?" Da-Bo raises a valid concern.

"Look at this card and tell me what it says," K-9 challenges Da-Bo.

(Looking at the card) "It says Jack Blake," Da-Bo responds, reading the name.

"You dumb motherfucker! You can't read for real?" K-9 taunts, pointing out Da-Bo's error.

"It says John Blake, not Jack. No one calls him John, and anyone who sees this will not think twice about it being his. This is the perfect time for us to pull this off, and I'm not going to pass it up," K-9 said.

Da-Bo looked skeptical. "Then why do we need a gun?"

K-9 grinned. "I'm not planning on shooting anybody. If we can't pick the locks, we will just shoot them off."

Inside Jack's office at the prison, Jack spoke into the phone, a clear sense of relief evident in his voice. "Jerry, could you please send someone to come and get these beds out of my office?"

Jerry's voice crackled through the receiver. "I know you're glad to be getting your office back from those two clowns. HA! HA!"

Jack chuckled. "You're right, and I hope that I will never see them again in here!"

Jerry's voice turned serious. "I don't want to disappoint you, sir, but with those two guys, I wouldn't count on it."

Jack sighed. "Well, let's hope for the best anyway."

Inside Da-Bo's friend's house, the atmosphere was dimly lit, casting shadows across the room. Da-Bo and K-9 found themselves amidst an assortment of guns, each one boasting its own lethal potential. With a hint of approval, K-9 pointed out a particular firearm that caught his attention and passed it over to Da-Bo's friend, signaling his preference.

"That'll be fifty dollars," Da-Bo's friend said.

K-9 urged Da-Bo to pay up. "Give it to him, Da-Bo."

Da-Bo reluctantly handed over the cash, muttering, "Alright, but you owe me."

Da-Bo's friend carefully wrapped up the gun and passed it to K-9.

The Keeper of the Castle

Outside Da-Bo's Friend's House

K-9 and Da-Bo walked briskly to their rented car and hopped in.

Outside Jack Blake's House

They arrived at their destination, Jack Blake's lavish residence.

"Do you think this is it?" K-9 asked, excitement in his voice.

Da-Bo pulled out the paper with Jack's address. "11324 Ranch Hill."

K-9 confirmed, "Sure is! Damn, man! Look at this house. I didn't know that people lived this good. Let's hurry up and break into this place because I know he has some valuable stuff in here."

They parked the car and stealthily made their way to the side of the house, where they found a way to enter. K-9 and Da-Bo were awestruck by the opulence that greeted them.

"We should've bought a truck and taken everything out of here. You think we can fit that big screen TV in the car?" Da-Bo remarked, eyeing the luxurious belongings.

K-9 chuckled. "I wish, but since we can't, let's grab what we can and get the hell out of here."

Da-Bo's eyes fell upon a family picture. "That must be his wife and kids."

K-9 couldn't help but leer. "Damn! Ain't she fine? This guy has it all. Hell, I don't even feel bad about what I'm doing now."

Inside the Kitchen

K-9 yanked a drawer off its hinges, causing it to crash onto the floor.

"Don't just stand there and watch me, dumbass. Go into the bedroom and see what you can find," K-9 barked at Da-Bo.

Da-Bo's actions were frenzied inside his bedroom, as he hastily pulled open dresser drawers, causing their contents to spill onto the floor in disarray.

Amid the chaos, his eyes widened with excitement as he stumbled upon a checkbook, a wad of $300 in cash, and valuable jewelry that glittered under the room's soft light.

Meanwhile, K-9 had ventured into the bedroom closet, where he swiftly gathered fur coats, leather jackets, and other luxurious garments, adding to their growing pile of loot. As they prepared to make their escape, K-9's keen memory triggered a realization— there was a high-quality sound system he had noticed earlier, and it was too valuable to be left behind. Determined, he swiftly made his way back to secure the prized item before they left the scene.

"Get out of the car and help me take this sound system," K-9 commanded Da-Bo.

Da-Bo protested, "Man, we got enough. Let's get the hell out of here!"

K-9's persistence kicked in. "Come on, punk! With you helping me, it won't take long."

They reluctantly returned to the house. Unbeknownst to them, LaDonna and the kids had just arrived and were approaching the house.

V

Da-Bo and K-9 found themselves laden with the weight of their ill-gotten gains inside the house. As they made their way through the dimly lit rooms, their senses heightened, and they tensed at the sound of approaching voices, indicating that they were not alone.

"Somebody is out there," K-9 whispered a sense of urgency in his voice.

Da-Bo panicked. "You see what happens when you get greedy? Now we're busted! How can we go back to prison for this after he let us out? It's bad enough getting busted, but out of all the houses, we choose his to get caught in."

K-9 tried to calm him down. "Shut up, and let's hide in this closet."

LaDonna and the kids entered the house. Jack Jr. walked away, unknowingly getting closer to K-9 and Da-Bo's hiding spot.

"Hey, baby! I'm home," LaDonna called out, unaware of the danger lurking nearby.

Linda, their daughter, spoke up. "Maybe he didn't hear you, Mommy."

But Jack Jr., their son, overheard their conversation and interrupted. "Well, one reason he didn't hear you is because his car is not in the garage."

LaDonna's suspicions were aroused. "Jack Jr., did you unlock the door?"

Jack Jr. denied responsibility. "No! It was already unlocked."

Fear and anger swept over LaDonna. "Why in the hell didn't you tell me? Quick, everybody out of the house!"

As LaDonna turned around, K-9 and Da-Bo found themselves face-to-face with her.

"Please, please take whatever you want, but don't hurt my kids or me," LaDonna pleaded, clutching her children tightly.

K-9, smirking, responded, "We're not going to hurt you, but when we leave, will you promise not to call the police?"

LaDonna, desperate to protect her family, agreed, "Yes, I promise. I will do anything, but please don't hurt us."

K-9's tone turned menacing. "You're a lying bitch!" He slapped her across the face.

Jack Jr., unable to bear witnessing his mother's mistreatment, stood up to K-9. "Leave my mother alone, punk!"

K-9 issued a warning. "You do what I say, and I might let you all go."

LaDonna nodded, tears streaming down her face. K-9 grabbed her, his intentions clear.

"Hey, man," K-9 called out to Da-Bo.

Da-Bo responded, "What?"

K-9 leered at LaDonna. "She sure is fine, ain't she? Look at her."

K-9 forcefully kissed LaDonna and violated her personal space. LaDonna cried silently, overwhelmed by terror and helplessness.

K-9, still fixated on his twisted desires, commanded Da-Bo, "Watch these two kids. I'm getting ready to have some fun."

As K-9 pulled out his gun and led LaDonna into the bedroom, Da-Bo was left to control Jack Jr. and Linda. The sounds of a horrendous assault reached their ears, causing Linda to cry even harder and Jack Jr. to struggle against Da-Bo's grip.

"Shut up, you little bitch, and hold still you little punk," Da-Bo hissed at them, resorting to violence to maintain control.

Da-Bo emerged from the bedroom, a sinister smile playing on his lips. "Come on, man, let's go."

K-9 paused for a moment. "Wait a minute."

K-9 dragged Linda and Jack Jr. into the bedroom with their mother and callously shot all three of them, ending their lives.

Da-Bo, witnessing the escalating brutality, realized the gravity of their actions. "What was supposed to be a robbery has turned into rape and murder."

Da-Bo turned towards the exit. "Fuck that damn thing; let's get the hell out of here."

As Da-Bo stepped outside, he noticed a woman running towards her car.

"Oh shit, K-9, we are in trouble now!" Da-Bo exclaimed, a sense of impending doom taking hold.

K-9 hurriedly joined Da-Bo, his eyes scanning the scene. "What are you talking about?"

Da-Bo pointed out the woman on her cell phone, getting into her car. "Look out here. You see that woman on the cell phone, pulling off? I bet she heard the gunshots."

Fear gripped K-9 and Da-Bo as they realized their heinous acts were not going unnoticed. Their initial excitement and confidence gave way to panic. They made a hasty retreat, running out of the house.

VI

Inside her car, the woman's heart pounded like a drumbeat of terror. Moments ago, she had hurriedly departed from the warden's house, only to be startled by the unmistakable sound of gunshots that echoed in the air. Fear gripped her tightly, and her instincts took over as she fumbled to make a frantic call, desperate to seek help and ensure her safety.

"I just left the warden's house, and I heard gunshots. Please send the police to 11324 Ranch Hill!" she pleaded to the operator.

Within the Police Station the police dispatcher's voice echoed through the station. "All available units to the warden's house at 11324 Ranch Hill. There is a reported shooting."

A police officer, half a block away, responded urgently, sitting in the police car. He spoke into the radio, requesting backup as he turned on his sirens and lights, racing towards the scene.

K-9 and Da-Bo, trapped in their rented car, watched in frustration as the police car pulled up behind them outside Jack's house

The police officer issued a stern command through the loudspeaker. "Get out of the car with your hands up in the air!"

Da-Bo and K-9 felt their anger and frustration building inside the Rent-a-Car.

"Now, what in the hell are we going to do?" Da-Bo asked, exasperated.

K-9, fueled by desperation, responded, "Shoot our way out of it!"

More police cars arrived outside Jack's home, surrounding them.

Da-Bo's frustration boiled over. "I guess you're going to outshoot all of them?"

K-9, surveying the growing number of officers, made a sobering decision. "Well, let's do it like the man said. Get out with your hands in the air."

Da-Bo sneered at K-9. "You bastard! I just messed up a good chance fucking around with your ass. I knew I shouldn't have listened to you."

K-9 and Da-Bo reluctantly obeyed, stepping out of the car with their hands raised. The police swiftly approached, ready to apprehend them. One officer, however, entered Jack's house, unaware of the gruesome scene that awaited him.

Inside the Prison Jack sat at his desk, engrossed in paperwork, when David burst through his office door.

"What in the hell is going on, David? You come crashing through my door like that," Jack exclaimed, taken aback.

David's face revealed urgency. "Come on, sir. Something has happened at your house, and we have to leave immediately."

Jack's heart raced as he grabbed his coat. Excitement and nervousness mingled within him. "What's going on?"

David's tone conveyed a mixture of concern and uncertainty. "I really don't know, but we must hurry. I left Jerry in charge."

Without further hesitation, Jack and David rushed out of the office, their minds filled with worry and unanswered questions.

There are nine police cars with their lights flashing and two crime unit trucks. Police are standing outside of the house. David and Jack are pulling up, and Jack hops out of the passenger's side.

"What's happening here?" Jack asks, running towards the house.

A policeman stops him, saying, "I am sorry, sir, but you can't go in there."

"The hell I can't! I'm the warden, and this is my house," Jack retorts, shaking himself loose as the policeman lets him go. He runs into the house.

Inside Jack's house, the bedroom was now a somber scene. Detectives carefully examined the room for evidence, while photographers meticulously documented every detail. In the midst of this grim environment, Jack rushed in, his face etched with anguish and disbelief.

His worst fears were realized as he saw his wife's lifeless form lying naked on the bed, bearing the tragic marks of gunshot wounds. The sight was devastating, and Jack was overcome with grief and shock at the sudden loss of his beloved partner. The room filled with an air of sorrow, and the weight of the tragedy hung heavily upon everyone present.

"NO!" Jack yells out, falling to the bedside, crying, and screaming.

"This can't be. Who did this and why?" Jack's voice trembles as a detective named Lou Baker comes to his aid, helping him up.

"I'm Detective Lou Baker of homicide, and your wife was just murdered and raped by the two guys you let out today," Lou explains somberly.

Jack, still crying, asks, "I don't understand. Where did they get the car and the gun from so quickly?"

"We found this on them," Lou shows Jack the credit card, adding, "We believe that is how they were able to get these things."

"That is my credit card. How in the hell did they get that?" Jack realizes with concern.

"They must have gone through my wallet when I stepped out of the office," Jack speculates.

"Do you keep your driver's license in your wallet?" Lou inquires.

"Yes, I do," Jack confirms.

"Well, that explains how they knew where you lived," Lou says.

"I can't believe this is happening. This can't be real. My kids, where are they?" Jack is in total shock, and Lou puts a hand on his shoulder, shaking his head.

"I'm sorry, Sir; they were murdered along with your wife," Lou delivers the heartbreaking news.

Overwhelmed, Jack calls for help, and Lou instructs one of his men to take Jack to the hospital, recognizing that he is on the verge of a nervous breakdown.

VII

Outside Jack's house, Lou spotted David from a distance and approached him with purpose. Extending his hand, he introduced himself as Lou Baker from the homicide division. As he got closer, he couldn't help but notice David's uniform, which led him to deduce that he worked for Mr. Blake.

"Could you tell me who is next in command at the joint?" Lou inquires.

"I am. My name is David Jones, and I am head of security. Could you please tell me what's going on?" David asks, deeply concerned.

"Well, your boss' family was murdered, and his wife was raped and killed by those two guys you all let out today," Lou reveals the horrifying truth.

"Oh hell no!" David exclaims in disbelief.

"I'm afraid so. Because of who he is and since he is in the hunt for governor, and the election is two weeks away, I'm going to keep him under tight surveillance for a couple of days. So that means you're going to be in charge until we release him. Under these circumstances, we don't want a bunch of reporters bugging him, and we want to make sure he doesn't have a nervous breakdown. He hasn't gotten over the shock yet, and I'm not sure how long it's going to take. Here is my number. Give me a call, and I'll let you know what's going on," Lou explains, offering David his contact information.

David agrees, and they shake hands. However, Lou stops before leaving and shares a somber thought with David.

"David, you know Mr. Blake well, don't you?" Lou inquires.

"Fairly well, why?" David asks curiously.

"If he decides to stay in the race for governor and he wins, you know that the rehabilitation program is going right out the window," Lou states sadly.

"I knew that from the start," David replies knowingly.

"Yeah! So did I, but it's too bad that it took something like this before Warden Blake figured it out. Well, take it easy and give me a call," Lou concludes, walking away. David remains standing there, holding Jack's credit card in his hand.

Inside the prison's lively recreation room, an array of activities filled the space. Groups of prisoners engrossed themselves in games of cards and checkers, while others congregated around the television. Two white inmates, Deliverance and Executioner, stood out from the crowd,

The Keeper of the Castle

their attention riveted on the news broadcast where K-9 and Da-Bo unexpectedly appeared on the screen.

Outside Jack's house, the situation was markedly different. The area was ablaze with the flashing lights of nine police cars and two crime unit trucks, creating an ominous glow against the night sky. Officers busied themselves with their duties, their stern faces and hurried movements indicating the gravity of the situation.

Nine police cars with their lights flashing and two crime unit trucks surround Jack's house. Police officers are on the scene as David and Jack arrive, pulling up to the house. Jack quickly hops out of the passenger's side, his concern evident.

"What's happening here?" Jack inquires, rushing towards the house.

A policeman stops him, saying, "I am sorry, sir, but you can't go in there."

"The hell I can't! I'm the warden, and this is my house," Jack retorts, shaking himself loose as the policeman relents, allowing him to enter the house.

Inside the bedroom, detectives and photographers are busy with their investigation. Jack rushes in, his heart sinking as he sees his wife lying naked on the bed, the tragic victim of gunshots.

"NO!" Jack cries out in despair, collapsing beside the bed, overcome with grief and anguish.

"This can't be. Who did this and why?" Jack's voice trembles as Detective Lou Baker approaches, offering his support and help.

"I'm Detective Lou Baker of homicide, and your wife was just murdered and raped by the two guys you let out today," Lou reveals, a somber expression on his face.

Unable to comprehend the swift turn of events, Jack cries, "I don't understand. Where did they get the car and the gun from so quickly?"

"We found this on them," Lou shows Jack the credit card, explaining, "We believe that is how they were able to get these things."

"That is my credit card. How in the hell did they get that?" Jack realizes with concern.

Realizing the unfortunate possibility, Jack contemplates, "They must have gone through my wallet when I stepped out of the office."

Lou further clarifies, "Do you keep your driver's license in your wallet?"

"Yes, I do," Jack confirms, understanding how they knew where he lived.

Overwhelmed by the devastating news, Jack's emotions surge, and Lou calls for help. Another officer takes Jack out of the house, helping him through the overwhelming tragedy.

Outside Jack's home, Lou notices David, approaches him, and introduces himself as Lou Baker of homicide, noticing David's uniform indicating he works for Mr. Blake.

"Could you tell me who is next in command at the joint?" Lou asks, seeking information.

"I am. My name is David Jones, and I am head of security. Could you please tell me what's going on?" David inquires, deeply concerned.

Lou delivers the shocking revelation, "Well, your boss' family was murdered, and his wife was raped and killed by those two guys you all let out today."

David reacts with disbelief, exclaiming, "Oh hell no!"

With the upcoming elections in mind, Lou explains, "I'm going to keep him under tight surveillance for a couple of days. So that means you're going to be in charge until we release him. Under these circumstances, we don't want a bunch of reporters bugging him, and we want to make sure he doesn't have a nervous breakdown. He hasn't gotten over the shock yet, and I'm not sure how long it's going to take."

David agrees, and they exchange contact information. However, Lou can't help but share a somber thought with David.

"David, you know Mr. Blake well, don't you?" Lou inquires.

"Fairly well, why?" David asks curiously.

Lou expresses concern, "If he decides to stay in the race for governor and he wins, you know that the rehabilitation program is going right out the window."

"I knew that from the start," David replies knowingly.

"Yeah! So did I, but it's too bad that it took something like this before Warden Blake figured it out. Well, take it easy and give me a call," Lou concludes, walking away, leaving David standing with Jack's credit card in his hand.

VIII

Inside the prison's rec room, prisoners engage in various activities, including playing cards, checkers, and watching TV. Two white prisoners, Deliverance and Executioner, are watching the news, and K-9 and Da-Bo appear on the screen.

"Hey everybody, come and look at this. It is K-9 and Da-Bo," Deliverance announces excitedly.

Everyone rushes over to the TV, including the guards, who turn up the volume at Executioner's request.

On the full-screen TV, the newscaster reports the shocking news, "Hello! My name is Robert Hannon, and our top story is about two inmates, just released from prison this morning, will find themselves back in jail again for robbery, rape, and murdering Jack Blake's family. Jack Blake is the warden of the Missouri State Department of Corrections, and he is the one that set them free!"

The prisoners react emotionally, with Hen J expressing disbelief, "They raped her!"

Deliverance responds bitterly, "You can't believe it. Just think how that punk-ass warden feels because he is the one that set them free. His family would still be alive if it wasn't for him."

Executioner laments the consequences, "We're never getting out of here now, and kiss better living conditions goodbye."

But Deliverance remains somewhat optimistic, "Not really. He is weak. The warden will cry for a month and then try to work things out."

Mutt Dog, offended by Deliverance's attitude, angrily interjects, "Motherfucker! Are you crazy? This man just lost his family, and you make it sound like someone just ran over his dog. Do all of you white boys think that'cause we're black, we don't have feelings?"

Tempers flare, and the guard steps in to prevent further escalation, warning that they'll be sent to the hole if they don't calm down.

The conversation shifts, and the guard warns them about the potential consequences of the warden's return.

Deliverance still appears optimistic, but Mutt Dog shares a bleak prediction, "Maybe he doesn't know, but I know. I shouldn't be saying this because I am black and in the penitentiary, but we are going to see the niggah come out in him!"

Inside the St. Luke's West Hospital, a solemn atmosphere fills Jack's private room. Jack sits attentively while a doctor stands nearby, engaged in a serious conversation. Despite the camera's proximity, the words exchanged between them remain muted, leaving the audience to observe their expressions and body language.

The doctor's concerned demeanor and Jack's thoughtful reactions convey the gravity of the discussion taking place. The room is adorned with medical equipment, and outside the window, the hospital's surroundings blur by as life continues its hurried pace. Inside the confined space, a sense of uncertainty prevails, with both Jack and the doctor grappling with the weight of the situation.

The scene captivates viewers, drawing them into the emotional intensity of the moment and prompting them to wonder about the outcome of this significant exchange within the walls of the hospital room.

David steps out of the elevator in the hospital hallway, accompanied by the Staff Doctor of Corrections, Otis Bush. Detective Lou Baker approaches, and they prepare to enter Jack's room when Lou stops them.

"Sorry, David, but you can't go in now. Jack is talking to the doctor," Lou informs them.

David asks, "How long do you think it will be before he is ready to leave?"

"Oh! A few minutes," Lou replies.

David introduces Otis to Lou, stating, "Otis, this is Detective Lou Baker. He was on the scene of Jack's family murders. Lou, this is our chief physician on staff, Otis Bush."

Pleasantries are exchanged, but Otis questions why he wasn't allowed to see Jack earlier. Lou explains that this is a police matter, and they prefer to conduct their evaluations without outside interference.

As Jack emerges from his room, Otis immediately approaches and embraces him with joy, asking, "Jack, my boy, how are you feeling?"

"About as well as can be expected," Jack responds, smiling weakly.

David offers to carry Jack's bag, and they discuss funeral arrangements. To Jack's surprise, David reveals that the expenses have been taken care of by a funeral home that previously contributed to his campaign.

Otis, observing Jack closely, notices something amiss, asking directly, "Jack, did you forget about the governor's race?"

Jack avoids the question initially, but Otis keeps a keen gaze on him. Eventually, Jack responds, "No. Of course not. I'm thinking about the funeral home. Come on, David, you ready to go?"

As they leave, Otis watches Jack closely until he is out of sight. Otis then approaches the doctor who was with Jack, possibly seeking more insight into Jack's emotional state.

Otis Bush, a doctor, approached Dr. Jonathan Milbrook.

"My name is Otis Bush, I'm a doctor," he introduced himself.

Dr. Milbrook replied, "My name is Jonathan Milbrook, and I'm pleased to meet you."

Curious about Jack's condition, Otis asked, "Please tell me, Dr. Milbrook, did you recommend to Jack that he should drop out of the governor's race, or did you say it to anyone else?"

"No, I didn't, and I don't see any reason why he should," Dr. Milbrook responded.

Otis was excited and exclaimed, "What! You've got to be kidding. This man is in no shape to be going back to work, let alone trying to run for governor!"

Dr. Milbrook tried to justify his decision, "I understand the mental state he's in, but my personal opinion is that he is fine. As a matter of fact, he's handling it better than I thought he would. He cried like a baby for the first day, and then the second day he was fine. We talked, and he seemed to be as intelligent as ever, and today, when I talked to him, he was the same way. So I decided to release him."

Concerned, Otis tried to make him see the change in Jack's behavior. "Doctor, can't you see that dramatic change in his behavior? That should be telling you something."

Dr. Milbrook inquired, "Something like what?"

Otis expressed his belief, "I believe that Jack is going to start suffering from post-traumatic stress syndrome if he hasn't already."

Skeptical, Dr. Milbrook questioned him, "What makes you so sure?"

Drawing from his experience, Otis explained, "I'm an expert in the field. When I was a young intern in the Vietnam War, most of the vets suffered from this disease because of shell shock. Now that I've been a doctor at the correctional center, 95% of the inmates I see suffer from this illness because of the rough lifestyles they lived growing up in tough, inner cities. A lot of them are shell-shocked, not because of the war, but because of what happened to them at home, on the streets, and at school—what they saw with their own eyes."

Dr. Milbrook remained doubtful, "So! What does this have to do with Jack? He is a very intelligent man and accepts reality. I know it's going to be hard for him, but I don't think he's going to go off the deep end like you're suggesting. Besides, he's never been in any of those situations you're talking about."

Otis tried to emphasize his point, "Never until now. Didn't you even notice how he reacted when I asked him about the governor's race? I really believe he forgot about it completely. I could see it in his eyes."

Dr. Milbrook tried to reason, "Come on, Doctor, give it a rest. For his sake, can't you understand that this man just lost his immediate family by a murder that he himself could have prevented?"

Undeterred, Otis insisted, "Doctor, maybe I am explaining myself wrong, but what I'm trying to say is that if this man runs for governor and wins, he could become a very dangerous man."

Dr. Milbrook sought clarification, "How do you figure that?"

Otis presented his concerns, "For one thing, he has the IQ of a genius and he graduated at the top of his class at Harvard. He's a lawyer and knows the law better than the people who made it. You give a man with this type of intelligence this much power, and he's suffering from this disease, all hell could break loose in Missouri."

Dr. Milbrook probed further, "All hell! Like what?"

Otis explained his fears, "That's the part that scares me because I never dealt with anyone with this kind of intelligence and power who suffers from posttraumatic stress syndrome. I just know that you'll see a big change."

Dr. Milbrook defended his decision, "Did it ever cross your mind, Doctor, that he might have enough intelligence to overcome this? Until you give me something a little more concrete, my decision stands. Mr. Blake is free to do whatever he wants. Have a good day, Mr. Bush."

Dr. Milbrook walked away, leaving Otis standing there shaking his head.

On Sunday morning, in the graveyard, everyone was leaving. Jack, his parents, Jerry, and David, were heading for the limousine. Jack walked his mother and father to the limousine that was behind the one he was getting into.

"Now, son, don't be afraid to call on us anytime, day or night. I know it's got to be rough," Jack's father comforted him.

Jack's mother added, "Yes, Jack, we'll always be here for you. Everyone will understand if you back out of the governor's race. You could always run again, and I know the pressure on you must be enormous."

Jack's mother gave him a hug, but Jack showed no emotion. His mother let go, wiping tears from her face.

"Don't you all worry about me; I'm all cried out. I'll run for governor and win just to make sure that this doesn't happen to anyone else again," Jack declared, holding his mother's hand and looking her in the eye.

"Please son, just promise me that you won't try to take the world's problems on your shoulders if you become governor," Jack's mother pleaded.

"That's right son. I know you're hurting, but it's only so much you can do," added his father.

Jack, showing no emotion and looking his father in the eye while still holding his mother's hand, responded firmly, "No! There is a lot I can do, and I'm going to do it. I will not shed another tear. Just like in the bible, Job had his whole family taken from him, and later, the Lord blessed him with more, and I feel that God will do the same for me."

Upon hearing Jack's words, his mother started crying again and hugged him tightly. Jack then walked his mother and father to their limousine and opened the door for them.

Meanwhile, Otis was running toward them, yelling, "Blake! Blake!"

Jack's father noticed him and asked, "Is that Otis?"

"Yes, it is," Jack replied.

Otis reached them and gave Jack's father a big hug, saying, "I thought you were going to get away from me before I had a chance to see you."

Jack's father explained, "Well, everything happened so quickly that we arrived in town hours before the funeral. I'm glad I got the chance to see you because we're heading to the airport right now."

Jack then addressed his mother and father, "Well, I know that you two have a lot to catch up on, so I'll be going."

He gave his mother and father a hug and added, "I will see you back at work, Otis, sometime next week."

Concerned for Jack, Otis asked, "Jack, are you sure you don't need any more time off?"

Jack smiled a little and replied, "No! Life must go on, and Mom and Dad, call me as soon as that plane lands to let me know you all made it safely."

With that, Jack walked back to his limousine, where David and Jerry were waiting for him. David opened the door for Jack, and all three of them got into the limousine, which then pulled off.

Otis expressed his concern to Jack's father, "I'm worried about your son, Blake."

Jack's father acknowledged, "Yes, I know. We all are, but he'll be alright."

Otis clarified, "No! That's not what I meant."

Perplexed, Jack's father asked, "Well! What do you mean, Otis?"

Otis revealed his suspicions, "I think your son is suffering from post-traumatic stress syndrome."

Jack's father tried to understand, "Are you talking about what some of those guys suffer from when the war is over?"

Otis confirmed, "Yes, I am. I think that Jack has been shocked that bad, and I'm scared of what he might do if he should become Governor."

Jack's father considered the situation, "Well! What do you want me to do, try and talk him out of it? If that is what it is, I'll be wasting my time. Jack has his mind made up, and I'll admit, he is taking this just a little too well for me also. But we just finished discussing that issue before you came up here."

Otis persisted, "Well! Couldn't you try, Blake?"

Jack's father explained, "No, I can't, but that doesn't mean that I disagree with you. Otis, I think you might just be right, but how can I tell an adult who hasn't lived under my roof in twenty years what he should and should not do? And he makes more money than I do and has put himself in a position that not only me but also most black people living can only dream about. I'm sorry, Otis, but there's nothing I can do."

Otis remained concerned, "Well, something needs to be done because he should not become Governor in his state of mind."

Jack's father questioned, "What state of mind? He doesn't act crazy, and he doesn't talk crazy. As a matter of fact, he has his own mother convinced that there's nothing wrong, and she knows him better than anybody. The only reason I can see your point is that I was in the war and learned a little about this myself. Most people, hell, I would say about 95% of the people in the United States, never heard of post-traumatic stress syndrome. If you're going around telling people that he's suffering from this, when they can see that he still has all of his senses, they're going to think that you're crazy! Besides, I heard that Senator John Beck is leading in the polls. He probably won't win anyway."

Otis bid farewell, "Well, my good friend, I know you have a plane to catch, and I hope the next time I see you, it'll be under happier circumstances."

"I hope so too, Otis. See you later," Jack's father replied.

"Goodbye, Blake. (Talking to Jack's mother) Don't let this guy give you a hard time. HA! HA!" Otis said to Jack's mother.

"I won't. He knows what'll happen if he tries. See you later, Otis," Jack's mother responded.

Jack's mother and father got into the limousine, and it pulled off.

Inside Jack's limousine, Jack and David sat next to each other, and Jerry sat across from them.

Jerry brought up the political situation, "Warden, Sir, you know that John Beck is taking a commanding lead in the polls? It's also rumored that Mayor Al Hopgood of St. Louis is moving in his favor."

Jack responded, "Well, I understand that some people have lost a little faith in me, but that can all change because I have changed!"

David offered his assistance, "Do you need me to come and pick you up next week, Sir, for the debates?"

"No, that's okay. Carl's going to pick me up. You two just meet me there," Jack replied.

IX

Inside the hotel ballroom, where the debates were taking place, Senator John Beck stood next to some of his supporters, including Mayor Al Hopgood of St. Louis. On the other side, Jack stood with some of his supporters, and Carl was right next to him. Reporters from various media outlets were setting up and reporting on the event.

The master of ceremonies called for the candidates to take their positions on the stage. Jack was the first one on stage and stood in the middle. Alex Randolph, the Republican nominee, was on the left, largely forgotten. John Beck was to be on Jack's right but had not made it to the stage yet.

John Beck confided in one of his supporters, "I'm going to eat this guy alive! I'm going to start off with his family situation and then throw it up in his face about trying to rehabilitate prisoners. And then I'm going to tell the good people of Missouri that if he let it happen to his own family, he sure as hell will let the same thing happen to theirs. No matter how good of a financial wizard he might happen to be, can he make enough money to bring his family back from his own stupid decisions?"

Some of Beck's supporters questioned his approach, "Don't you think that is a little uncalled for, considering that his family was murdered less than two weeks ago?"

Overhearing the conversation, Mayor Al Hopgood joined in, "This is politics. Anything and everything goes! You have to do whatever you can to get the edge, even if it means hurting somebody mentally or physically!"

"I agree. You can't be Mr. Nice Guy, or you will get screwed. Besides, I don't want a governor who lets prisoners in the front door and then, when nobody is looking, he lets them out the back door," John Beck asserted.

John Beck left his supporters and took his place on the stage, standing to the right of Jack. The master of ceremonies called for the debates to begin with the first question directed to Warden Blake.

Jack interrupted, "I know what you're going to ask."

Inside the prison, Mutt Dog and the guard who stopped him from fighting earlier in the week watched the debates with interest.

Mutt Dog asked, "Anybody want to watch the warden?"

Someone in the prison shouted, "Awe! Fuck him!"

Back inside the ballroom, the debates continued, and Jack started addressing the crowd, "I know that a lot of people have lost faith in me that did support me. This is one reason that I'm here tonight. I want to try to gain that support back from the politicians and the Missouri voters. I did something that every one of us has done at least one time in our lives (Intense), and that is, I made a mistake! That mistake turned out to be a very big sin! I promise that it will not happen again! (Continuing) If I'm elected governor, I'm going to tell you all something that is not false but true. What happened to me and my family? I'm going to make damn sure that it doesn't happen to any of you! Can you all understand? You know what a financial wizard I am? Tell me, you good people of Missouri, do you want to hear my plan?"

The ballroom was electrified as Jack raised his arms in the air, and the crowd erupted in cheers. On the other hand, John Beck wore a nervous expression, clearly feeling the pressure.

Inside the prison, Mutt Dog and the guard watched the TV closely, intrigued by the unfolding events.

Jack, with confidence, addressed the crowd, "I'm going to make it quick and right to the point. We can't continue to spend the taxpayer's money on these no-good people locked up in the joint! It costs $100,000 a cell block, $25,000 a prisoner, and $20 million alone in drug rehabilitation, not counting healthcare coverage! With the 13 prisons and local jails, the taxpayers are spending close to a billion dollars a year. Is this what you all want?"

The crowd responded passionately, "NO! NO!"

"Is this right?" Jack questioned.

Again, the crowd responded emphatically, "NO! NO!"

Jack continued, "If I am elected governor, I promise, as long as my name is Jack, the taxpayers of Missouri will not have to spend that much money on something as dumb as that, and that is a matter of fact! Now here is the plan: The day I take office if elected, I will start executing every prisoner on death row, and I want to include child molesters and rapists on this list. I'm going to do it cheaper than the gas chamber, the electric chair, and the lethal injection. As a matter of fact, it will only cost five cents a prisoner; we're saving $25,000. I'll execute one a day and maybe even two, depending on how I feel. In one week's time, the taxpayer will have spent a total of thirty-five cents; you would have saved $175,000. Can you live with that?"

The crowd enthusiastically responded, "YES! YES!"

Jack continued to lay out his plan, "If you can live with that, then you sure can live with this. In one year's time, the taxpayer will have spent $18.25; you would've saved $27,325,000. Not only are we executing prisoners, but we're also saving space. Now that we will have the space, we don't need to spend $6,000,000 on a new prison. Can you live with that?"

The crowd cheered again, "YES! YES!"

Jack took a moment to rally support, "So, who do you all want to see elected today? John Beck or John Blake? By the way, if you are my friend, you can call me Jack! If you want to see John Beck, then go out and vote for him. If you want to see me, let me hear everyone say,'TO HECK WITH BECK AND COME BACK JACK!'"

The crowd went wild, chanting in unison, "TO HECK WITH BECK AND COME BACK, JACK! TO HECK WITH BECK AND COME BACK JACK! TO HECK WITH BECK AND COME BACK JACK!"

Jack, with a wide smile and hands raised high, basked in the overwhelming support from the crowd. Supporters of John Beck tore up his posters and pennants, further solidifying Jack's position.

As John Beck witnessed the enthusiastic response, he approached Jack and raised Jack's hand in the air. Jack was puzzled, but John motioned that he wanted the microphone.

"Let me say something," John whispered to Jack.

Jack stepped aside, and John Beck addressed the crowd, "Hey! Hey! Come on with this heck with Beck stuff!"

The crowd grew even louder, some even booing him. John Beck signaled to Jack to come to the microphone, and Jack obliged.

"I would like to make an announcement. John Beck has just told me he's dropping out of the race for Governor," Jack declared.

The crowd erupted in cheers once more.

John Beck requested the opportunity to speak, and the crowd quieted down as he stepped up to the microphone. In the midst of the cheering, Otis Bush entered the room.

Not fully aware of the situation, Otis asked, "Hey, what's going on? I heard all the noise outside?"

Someone in the crowd told him to be quiet and listen.

Otis had a sudden realization, "Oh shit! No! This can't be!"

Some people in the crowd noticed Otis's reaction and engaged in conversation with him, wondering why he was so concerned.

John Beck explained to Otis, "I know I can't win, and I do not want to give up my position as Senator, and I don't want this heck with Beck to carry over when it's time for my reelection. So could you please make them shut up so I can say a few words to save my ass!"

Jack laughed heartily and nodded in agreement.

"I know what you mean. You would at least think they would have kept the shirt," John Beck said, noticing the banners and torn-up pictures of himself on the floor.

John Beck turned and started to walk away but then stopped and turned back to face Otis.

Meanwhile, the crowd continued to celebrate, and people walked on stage to shake Jack's hand and show their support.

Otis put his hand on John Beck's shoulder, and Beck turned around to face him.

"Excuse me, Senator, but I know I am out of line. My name is Otis Bush, and I am the chief physician at the Missouri State Department of Corrections. I've been acquainted with Warden Blake for a long time, and I feel he's suffering from a disease that not many people know about. If he's elected governor, we all could be headed for a lot of trouble," Otis earnestly conveyed.

John Beck responded with an attitude, "So! What in the hell do you want me to do about it?"

Otis tried to reason with him, "You're the only one that has a chance of beating him, and you're dropping out of the race. Why?"

"You must have just walked in, right, Mr...?" Beck struggled to remember Otis's name.

"Otis Bush," Otis reminded him.

"Yeah! Right, Otis! Well, friend, let me tell you what you've missed," Beck continued, "Your boss, the warden, has done a 360, that means he turned his whole campaign around! Instead of rehabilitating the prisoners, he's talking about killing them all! That was the only leg I had to stand on, and when he changed his mind, it was like he kicked that one from underneath me. So I'm getting out while I can. But don't take my word for it. If you think I still have a chance to win, go out there and ask some of the people in the crowd whom they want for governor. Better yet, look around. Do you see any of my pennants or banners hanging up anywhere?"

Otis looked around and realized that no one was holding a John Beck sign.

"Now look on the floor," John Beck added.

Otis looked on the floor and saw banners torn up along with pictures of John Beck for governor and some shirts.

Otis couldn't believe what he was seeing, "This can't be."

"I know what you mean. You would at least think they would have kept the shirt. HA! HA! Now you should be able to understand why I'm getting out of the race. Have a nice day, Sir," John Beck said, turning to leave.

As he walked away, he stopped and turned back to Otis, facing him once more.

John Beck, forgetting Otis's name again, asked, "Oh, by the way, um, um, what's your name again?"

"Otis," he replied.

"Yeah, right, Otis. You wouldn't mind a little friendly advice, would you?" John Beck inquired.

Otis was open to it, "No! Shoot."

"Now, what did you say the name of this strange disease is that you think the Warden has?" John Beck questioned.

"Post-traumatic stress syndrome," Otis answered.

"Yes, you're right. It is strange, and I've never heard of it. I'm pretty sure that most of the people in Missouri haven't heard of it either. But here is my advice- if I were you, I wouldn't be going around shooting my mouth off about a crazy disease that no one has heard of and trying to make it stick to Warden Blake. Personally, he looks good and sounds great to me, and that's the opinion of everybody who sees and talks to him. I'm afraid, my friend, if you continue to tell everyone that you think there's something wrong with Warden Blake, they're going to think that you're the one who's crazy. And, since he is your boss, you would be walking on dangerous ground. Have a nice day," John Beck advised.

After John Beck walked off, Otis stood there with a dumbfounded look on his face. He glanced up at the stage, where fans and reporters surrounded Jack Blake, who was shaking hands and talking, but the audio was inaudible from where Otis stood.

Otis turned around, feeling perplexed, and slowly walked out the door.

One week later, on Election Day, at 10:00 PM, Jack Blake's headquarters buzzed with excitement. Everybody gathered around the television, and reporters rushed in carrying microphones and cameras, surrounding Jack and eager to get his thoughts.

X

As the newscasters announced Jack's victory, he stood tall, ready to answer their questions. "It's official; Missouri has its first black Governor in history, and Jack Blake has become the second black Governor in the history of the United States. Now we're going to a live shot with our very own Stan Budworth, who's standing next to the Governor-elect. Take it away, Stan!" the newscaster declared.

Stan, the reporter, approached Jack with his microphone, "So, Warden, how does it feel knowing that you're going to be Governor, and do you still plan on carrying out the executions of every prisoner on death row?"

Jack replied with confidence, "Well, it feels great knowing that I'm going to be Governor, and yes, I'm going to carry out my plan to the fullest."

Stan continued to inquire, "A lot of people have asked me how you're going to execute the prisoners without using the chair, gas, or lethal injection."

Jack tantalized the audience, "Well, I'm going to let that be a surprise. And I promise my new method of execution will have everybody thinking twice about pulling a gun out and shooting, raping, or molesting anyone. As a matter of fact, I guarantee it."

The reporter persisted, "So, when is the execution of the prisoners going to start?"

Jack responded, "The first day I'm in office, the only one who can stop the execution of a prisoner is the governor, right?"

"That's right, Sir," Stan confirmed.

Jack added, "Now that I'll soon be Governor, I'm not stopping any executions, and I'll give you all a hint about how I'm planning on doing it. I'm going to be the one that sets the timer and presses the button."

Stan was intrigued, "Setting a timer and pressing a button, what are you talking about, Sir?"

Jack teased, "Think about it."

Stan laughed, but then a serious look crossed his face, "You're not talking about using a microwave, are you?"

"That's exactly what I'm talking about, and I must add that I won't always be the one setting the timer or pressing the button," Jack revealed.

Stan seemed taken aback, "Well, I know that, Sir. Your guards will do some of the executions?"

"No, they will not! What I'm talking about doing is getting in contact with the people who lost their family members to these prisoners and letting them set the timer and press the button. That way, some of the good people of Missouri can get revenge without having to go to jail for it. And they can feel justice has been served!" Jack explained passionately.

Stan raised concerns, "But Sir, isn't that going a little far?"

"No, Stan, it is not, and I'll tell you why. When people realize that someone in their family has been murdered, the first thing they want to do is go out and kill that person who's responsible. Now, instead of one murder, we have to solve two. This method will cut down on the revenge motive because everyone will know that they don't have to go out and kill anyone for justice to be served in their own mind. They know that they're going to get the chance to press the button and that they don't even have to worry about going to jail. Plus, that makes it easier for the police because that's one less retaliation case they have to worry about," Jack justified.

Stan was skeptical, "Do you really think that this'll work?"

Jack confidently replied, "Well, let me put it to you like this. I'm planning to show these executions live on TV! We all know that seeing is believing. It's sad that the most highly rated programs are violent yet make-believe. Just think of what an impact it will have when people tune in and know that this is real life—knowing that if you commit murder, child molestation, or rape in Missouri, this is going to be your outcome. I'm planning on showing it at least once a week. Just like people sit in front of the TV looking for lottery numbers, I'm going to have people sitting in front of their TV looking for the executions!"

Inside the prison's rec room, Mutt Dog, Deliverance, Executioner, Hen J, and other prisoners watched Jack on TV with interest. As Jack's message spread, the atmosphere in the room grew tense and full of emotions.

Hen J exclaimed, "Man! He can't be serious. Can he?"

The guard responded, "Why can't he?"

Executioner chimed in, "Where in the hell is he going to get a microwave that big?"

The guard retorted, "Well, if they can make one big enough to put popcorn in, I think they can make one big enough to fit your big ass inside of it."

As the prisoners discussed Jack's plans, Otis stood in the room, observing the situation quietly.

Meanwhile, inside Jack's headquarters, Jack and his friend Carl were engaged in a private conversation. Carl expressed concern, "Jack, are you going crazy with this microwave execution stuff? Have you lost your mind? And what about this TV? I know for a fact that you don't have any station that's going to televise it."

Jack took a seat in a chair, and Carl stood over him, awaiting an explanation.

"No, I'm not going crazy, and do me a favor. Make sure that the door is locked, and then I will explain," Jack requested.

Carl complied and locked the door.

Jack elaborated on his plans, "First, I'm going to contact TV stations if they don't contact me first. I know people want to see this, and so do the TV stations. They will even start bidding war against one another to get the rights to televise it. The best thing about it is that the taxpayers are not paying for the executions, and we're going to make a lot of money off of this."

Carl was still skeptical, "What makes you so sure that this is going to work?"

"Carl, if people tune in to watch all of those dumbass talk shows, you know they're going to tune in to watch a live execution, especially if you're doing it in a way they've never seen or heard of before, using a microwave," Jack replied confidently.

Still, Carl had reservations, "This is still not making any sense to me. Where in the hell are you going to get a microwave that's going to be big enough to fit people inside? It's not like you can go to K-Mart and pick up a life-size microwave."

"The microwave is already built. I'm just waiting on the finishing touches," Jack revealed.

Curious, Carl asked, "What finishing touches?"

Jack grinned, explaining, "The microwave is going to be equipped with a washer and grinder."

Carl seemed puzzled, "Don't you mean washer and dryer?"

"No! I mean a washer and a grinder! When I execute the prisoners in the microwave, no one is going to have to clean up. The microwave is going to have its own wash cycle, and the grinder is going to be for the bones that are left over. Let's just say if the families of the prisoners want a funeral service, it'll have to be a closed casket unless they want to show off some ground-up bones. HA! HA!" Jack revealed, displaying a sinister sense of humor.

Carl stared at Jack in disbelief, "What's wrong, Carl? Why are you looking at me like that?"

Carl voiced his concern, "Because I think that you are losing your mind. I know what you're going through with the loss of your family, but this is not right, plus…"

Jack cut Carl's conversation off, his anger boiling over. "How in the hell can you say you know what I'm going through? When was the last time someone in your family was murdered for no good damn reason? Tell me when?"

Carl remained silent, unable to comprehend the depth of Jack's pain.

"That's just what I thought. You can't begin to imagine the pain and hurt I feel unless it has happened to you," Jack continued, his frustration evident.

"Jack, I'm sorry, but all I'm trying to say is that some people will question this method of yours. I'm not sure that what you're talking about doing is legal," Carl replied, attempting to reason with him.

"Well, Carl, that's where you come in," Jack retorted, regaining some composure.

"What do you mean by that?" Carl inquired.

"I'm going to appoint you as the Official Prosecuting Attorney of the state of Missouri. And if there are going to be any questions asked, they're going to be asked by you, right?" Jack explained.

Carl hesitated, concerned about the pressure he might face from others. But Jack had an offer to sweeten the deal, "How much do you make a year?"

"I make $60,000," Carl replied.

"How does $100,000 a year sound to you?" Jack proposed, a sly smile forming on his face.

Carl's eyebrows raised in surprise, "Not bad. Not bad at all."

"Including the money we're going to make off of the prisoners, you may pull in a million dollars for the year, and we're going to make sure that it's all legal. So what do you think now?" Jack assured him.

"Well, you've got to love it," Carl smiled back, feeling enticed by the prospect.

Jack got up from his chair and approached Carl, giving him a hug. They were both smiling and laughing, thrilled about their potentially lucrative plan.

"Man! We're going to be rich, and it's going to be legal," Jack exclaimed with excitement.

Time passed, and the Governor's Mansion held a party to celebrate Jack's victory. Among the guests were representatives from various TV stations, including Harry Fishburn from KKOT, Wally Calhoun from WESU, and Ed Walker from KGO. They engaged in a bidding war to secure the rights to televise the microwave executions.

Jack took the TV reps to the basement to demonstrate the microwave execution. He placed a live turkey inside, showing them how the meat was blown off the bones in less than a minute. The gruesome but efficient process left the representatives astonished and intrigued by the prospect of broadcasting such events.

The bidding reached an astounding ten million dollars, and Harry Fishburn emerged as the winner. Jack was ecstatic about the lucrative deal and planned to use the money to fund the executions and cover other expenses.

However, a new challenge arose. Carl informed Jack that a law prohibited politicians from profiting from their own ideas, presenting a potential roadblock. Jack was adamant about changing the law and called for a meeting with all the members of the Senate and House of Representatives to convince them to amend the legislation.

Two days later, inside the Capitol Building, a heated discussion unfolded. Some politicians voiced concerns about the morality of Jack's execution method and questioned his intentions to profit from it. Jack assured them that the funds were entirely separate from taxpayer money and that he was willing to prove the source of the income. Nonetheless, opposition lingered, and some politicians remained skeptical.

One outspoken politician, Mr. Johnson, stood up to address Jack directly. "Governor Blake, I understand your intentions, but this method of execution raises serious ethical questions. We cannot allow the state to endorse such violence, even if it targets heinous criminals."

Jack listened carefully, recognizing the gravity of Mr. Johnson's arguments. "I understand your concerns, Mr. Johnson," he replied, "but we must also consider the plight of the victims' families. They have suffered unimaginable pain and loss. This method serves not just as punishment but also as a deterrent, ensuring that others think twice before committing such heinous acts."

Other politicians nodded in agreement, and the room fell silent, contemplating the implications of Jack's proposal. Jack continued, "I am willing to compromise. Let's establish a commission of experts and stakeholders to review and monitor the executions. Their task will be to ensure that the process remains just and that we do not overstep ethical boundaries."

Mr. Johnson looked thoughtful for a moment before responding, "I appreciate your willingness to consider oversight. That could alleviate some concerns. But we must be cautious, Governor, as we venture into uncharted territory."

Jack nodded, acknowledging the validity of Mr. Johnson's caution. "You have my word that I will be open to further discussions and amendments as needed. This is not about a personal vendetta; it's about taking decisive action against violent criminals while respecting the law."

As the debate continued, other politicians expressed varying opinions. Some were still skeptical, while others warmed up to the idea of the inclusion of an oversight commission. In the end, a majority agreed to support Jack's proposal, with the condition that the commission would have the authority to intervene if any ethical boundaries were crossed.

With the agreement in place, Jack's plan to implement the microwave executions with oversight became a reality. The first execution was scheduled for the following week, and the TV stations prepared to broadcast the event.

However, as the date approached, protests and controversies erupted throughout the state and the nation. Activists, human rights organizations, and some politicians vehemently opposed the new execution method. They argued that state-sanctioned violence was not the solution and that it would only perpetuate a cycle of revenge and brutality.

Amid mounting pressure, the oversight commission faced the daunting task of ensuring the execution process adhered to the strictest ethical standards. Jack and Carl found themselves navigating a storm of political challenges, moral dilemmas, and public outcry.

The fate of the microwave executions hung in the balance, and the nation watched closely as Missouri became the center of a deeply divisive and contentious debate. Jack's commitment to making a bold statement against violent crime clashed with the concerns for human rights and the potential consequences of his revolutionary approach.

"Well, Governor, what most of the people here want to know is what's in it for them if we pass this law?" Politician 3 said.

"So, is that the problem? What is in it for all of you?" Jack yelled at him.

"Yes, yes." The Crowd screamed with Jack.

XI

Governor Jack Blake stood on the stage, facing the crowd of politicians and eager citizens. The atmosphere was tense as the fate of the proposed law hung in the balance.

"Well, if you all pass this law and put it into effect immediately, I will have a check for $5,000 for each one of you, and you can pick it up as soon as you leave here after passing that bill. So what do you all think?" Jack asked, talking to Politicians 1 and 2.

"Well, now that I thought about it, maybe it is not so morally wrong after all." Politician 1 replied, looking at Jack.

"I agree. Hell, we're going to kill them anyway. We may as well get paid for it. HA! HA!" Politician 2 said, agreeing with the other politician.

"All in favor, say "aye," Jack said out loud.

"Aye," all the politicians yelled.

"All opposed," Jack said as he shrugged his shoulders.

Nobody says a word.

"All opposed," Jack said, looking at the crowd and then at the politicians.

In the tense silence that followed, Jack took note of the lack of objections and saw it as a positive sign.

A sense of satisfaction crossed his face as he broke the silence, saying, "Well, it looks like the'ayes' have it. Pass that bill, make it a law, and then go pick up your checks."

His remark carried a hint of confidence, pleased that his proposal seemed to have garnered support without any dissenting voices. As the weight of his words settled in the room, the scene left viewers curious about the implications of this decision and the consequences it might bring.

Carl expressed astonishment, "I can't believe you pulled this off."

As they walked towards the limousine, Carl continued, "One thing you must remember is most of the people in this world are greedy whether they know it or not. And we're dealing with politicians. I knew if I offered them some money, they would pass whatever I wanted. I'm just surprised that they sold out that cheap."

They both got into the limousine, and it pulled off.

Jack's voice echoed in the car, "Carl, I want you to get in contact with the local radio and TV stations and advertise that we're going to charge twenty-five dollars a head for anyone who wants to see this live. I want to turn this into an event. Oh, by the way, Carl, how does it feel to be a millionaire?"

Carl's voice responded enthusiastically, "Feels great, Sir! Man, this feels great!"

Inside Jack's office at the Missouri State Department of Corrections, David sits behind Jack's desk. As Jack walks in, David expresses excitement and gladness, "Governor Warden, Sir, it's good to see that you're finally back."

Jack warmly shakes David's hand and replies, "Thank you, David, and I want to commend you on the great job you've been doing. I know I said I was going to be back in a couple of days after I left the hospital, but I've just been so busy with other things. Plus, I needed the time off."

"Did you order us some new uniforms?" David turned to Jack and asked.

"Yes, I did, and where are they?" Jack responded, curious about the location of the uniforms.

"They're in the storeroom. I started to issue them out, but I noticed that they were military uniforms, and I wasn't sure if that was what you wanted," David explained, his excitement evident.

"That's exactly what I wanted. You see, David, this is a war, and I want everyone who steps in here to know it, especially the prisoners. Because they're prisoners of war for the crimes they committed on the streets. For murderers, the same thing is going to go for rapists and child molesters. When I get this law passed, we're taking no prisoners! They are all going straight to the microwave!" Jack exclaimed passionately.

David's eyes widened in surprise, and he asked, "You're not joking, are you, Sir? I had a chance to see the microwave, and that thing is huge! How big is it, eight by 6?"

"No, but close. It's eight by 6, and that means there's not a man or woman in this world that won't be able to fit inside it. I want everyone to know that Jack Blake means business!" Jack asserted confidently.

With a sudden realization, David said, "Oh yeah! I almost forgot this came by UPS."

Curious, Jack asked, "What is it?"

David handed over a box that was four by 1/2, and Jack eagerly opened it. He pulled out a large black nightstick with excitement, exclaiming, "Yes! I have been waiting for this. Just what I wanted. Feel this, David."

David hesitated slightly but held the nightstick in his hands, commenting, "This is really heavy, Sir."

Jack agreed, saying, "Yes, I know. Let me have it."

With the nightstick in his possession, Jack started walking around the office, swinging it like a madman, catching David's attention.

Jack's face bore a sinister grin as he swung the large black nightstick with an evil look in his eyes. David couldn't help but express concern about the potential damage it could cause.

"The way you're swinging that stick, Sir, if you hit a man on the leg, I bet it would break his leg," David nervously remarked.

"That's the whole idea! I believe that you're right, but there's one way to find out," Jack responded, clearly relishing the thought.

With a forceful strike, Jack brought the nightstick down hard on his desk, causing it to crack and pieces of wood to go flying. David's eyes widened, frozen in a mixture of fear and disbelief.

"Sir! Is everything all right?" David hesitated to ask, unsure of what to make of the display.

Jack's expression shifted from menacing to nonchalant, "Of course! Why would you ask?"

Trying to put David at ease, Jack started laughing, "Don't think that I'm going crazy, David, because I'm not. Just having a little fun. Besides, I'm having a new desk delivered today."

David took a breath, relieved by Jack's response, though still somewhat nervous. He decided to change the topic, "Well, Sir, I will go issue the new uniforms to the men."

As David turned to leave, Jack's voice boomed, "David! Did I say you could leave?"

Startled, David turned back to face Jack, "No Sir! You didn't. I'm sorry."

Jack continued to play with the nightstick, lightly hitting the desk as he said, "Come here, David. I got something for you."

Reluctantly, David approached Jack, unsure of what to expect. Jack reached into a drawer, pulled out an envelope, and set it on the top of the desk, pushing it towards David with the stick in his hand.

"Open it up, David, and tell me what you think?" Jack instructed.

David nervously grabbed the letter and opened it. His face lit up with happiness as he saw the contents, "Is this right, Sir! Fifty thousand dollars for me?"

"That's right, but be honest with me, David. Didn't you think for a moment that I might be losing my mind?" Jack inquired, trying to gauge David's reaction.

"I must admit you were acting kinda strange, but fifty thousand dollars! I can see that everything is all right! Thank you, Sir!" David exclaimed, genuinely grateful for the unexpected windfall.

"That's for the great job you did while I was gone," Jack said, expressing his gratitude to David. "When you issue the uniforms, tell Jerry to come up here and get his check too."

"Will do, Sir," David replied with a smile, pleased to receive Jack's acknowledgment.

Jack and David exchanged smiles, but as David leaves the room, Jack's smile quickly fades away, revealing the weight of his emotions.

Inside the prison, the next day, just before the executions were to begin, loud footsteps echoed through the corridors as cell doors slammed shut. The sound of someone yelling "turnkey!" filled the air, and then the door to the office opened.

In view, a group of men clad in black boots and army fatigues stood outside Jack's office. As Jack stepped out, he was dressed similarly in army fatigues, blending in with the guards, except for the black beret he wore. While the guards carried automatic guns, Jerry was among them, standing next to Jack.

"Are you ready, Sir?" Jerry asked Jack.

"Let's go," Jack replied with a determined look on his face.

XII

As Jack and the guards walked down the cellblock, the prisoners carried on with their usual commotion, but some of them noticed Jack's presence. It had been a while since they had seen him since the tragedy that befell his family.

In one of the cells, Prisoner 1 noticed Jack and whispered to his cellmate, "Man, is that the warden dressed up like that?"

Prisoner 2, overhearing the comment, replied with a smirk, "I don't know, but if it is, he looks just like GI JOE! HA! HA!"

As they continued down the cellblock, one prisoner's voice stood out among the rest. It was the same prisoner who had previously mocked Jack, calling him friendless.

"Hey warden! Hey warden!" the prisoner called out, seeking Jack's attention.

Jack and the guards approached the cell to see what the prisoner wanted. With an attitude, Jack asked, "What is it?"

The prisoner taunted, "The only thing I want to know is, how is the family? HA! HA!"

Laughter erupted from some of the other prisoners in nearby cells, as well as the prisoner's cellmates. Jack's expression turned dark as he stared at the prisoner, his anger evident.

"Open his cell door!" Jack ordered the guards, and they promptly dragged the prisoner out of the cell. Jack noticed the knee brace the prisoner was wearing.

"I can't tell you how my family is doing because they are dead," Jack coldly stated. "I can tell you how they might have felt before they were killed."

Without hesitation, Jack swung his nightstick with full force, hitting the prisoner's knee with the brace on it. A loud pop echoed as the knee broke, and the brace flew off. The prisoner cried out in pain, clutching his injured knee.

"You fucker! What the hell's wrong with you?" the prisoner screamed.

"This is what's wrong with me," Jack replied coldly. He swung the stick again, breaking the other knee, and the prisoner fell to the ground in agony, holding both knees.

"One day I'm gonna get your ass for this!" the prisoner cried.

Looking down at the prisoner, Jack sneered, "Oh really! Now that's no way for you to talk to your warden!" The fear in the prisoner's eyes was evident as Jack stood tall with his nightstick in hand.

Inside the prison, the loud footsteps and slamming cell doors fill the air as the guards, dressed in black boots and army fatigues, accompany Jack, who wears a black beret and carries the nightstick. Jerry is one of the guards accompanying Jack.

As they walk down the cellblock, the prisoners notice Jack's presence, and whispers start among them.

"Man, is that the warden dressed up like that?" Prisoner 1 asks his cellmate.

"I don't know, but if it is, he looks just like GI JOE! HA! HA!" Prisoner 2 chuckles.

Suddenly, one prisoner yells out to Jack, the same one who had taunted him before, seeking attention.

"Hey warden! Hey warden!" the prisoner calls out.

Jack and the guards approach the cell to confront the prisoner.

"What is it?" Jack asks, showing an attitude.

"The only thing I want to know is, how is the family? HA! HA!" the prisoner taunts, prompting laughter from others nearby.

Without a word, Jack orders the guards to open the prisoner's cell door. As the prisoner is dragged out, Jack notices the knee brace he is wearing.

"I can't tell you how my family is doing because they are dead. I can tell you how they might have felt before they were killed," Jack says coldly.

With a fierce swing of his nightstick, Jack hits the prisoner's knee with the brace on it. The knee breaks with a loud pop, and the prisoner cries out in pain.

"You fucker! What the hell's wrong with you?" the prisoner shouts.

"This is what's wrong with me," Jack responds, swinging the stick again, breaking the other knee.

The prisoners watching are alarmed, and their cellmates express their disapproval.

"That ain't right. You can't be doing us like that!" Cell Mate 1 protests.

"That's right! We gonna report you!" Cell Mate 2 adds.

Jack mocks their threat, "Oh yeah! Who are you going to report me to? The Governor?" He smiles and laughs a little.

To address the unruly prisoners, Jack walks to the center of the cellblock.

"Would everyone shut up!" Jack demands, but the prisoners continue to make noise. Frustrated, he runs to different cells, swinging his stick to get their attention.

"Now that I got you low-life, no good bums' attention, I want everyone to understand me and understand me good! I'm not taking no crap off any of you, and if I say do something, you all better damn well do it!" Jack warns, pointing to the injured prisoner. "If I say jump, don't ask how high, but how long do you want me to stay in the air? Because if you don't, you all will end up like him."

As the guards carry the injured prisoner back, the cellmates express concern for him. One suggests that he needs medical attention, but Jack responds harshly, breaking the inmate's wrist and hand with his nightstick. Jack threatens to deny him medical attention and warns the prisoners that they could be treated the same way.

Jack then instructs the guards to take the injured prisoner to the hole. Inside the hole, the prisoner pleads for forgiveness, mentioning their previous talk of friendship. He tries to appeal to Jack's empathy by mentioning they share the same name.

Instead, Jack smiles and presents the prisoner with a box containing rats.

"Maybe they will be your friends," Jack taunts, revealing the rats inside the box. The prisoner becomes terrified.

"Begging and crying, please don't, please don't do this!" the prisoner pleads.

Showing no emotion, Jack orders the guards to throw the prisoner into the hole with the rats.

The guards throw the prisoner inside the room, and there is no bed or restroom. The prisoner is lying on the floor helplessly with two broken kneecaps. Jack empties the box of rats on the prisoner and shuts the door. As Jack

The Keeper of the Castle

and the guards walk away, the prisoner is screaming at the top of his lungs.

"Please help me! These rats are biting me!" The prisoners screamed, asking for help.

"The backs of the guards and Jack as they walk down the hall. As they turn the corner, you can hear the cell door slam and the prisoner crying and yelling." Angle on replied.

The very next day, on the execution, there are some men working outside the prison. They are taking down the sign "Missouri State Department of Corrections" and putting up the "Missouri State Penitentiary" sign.

Inside the prison medical ward, Otis Bush, the prison doctor, is tending to one of the prisoners when the guards enter, carrying the prisoner that Jack had beaten up. Walking alongside them is the prisoner whom Jack had struck on the wrist and hands with his stick. Concerned, Otis rushes over to them.

"What happened to this man? Where is his knee brace I put on last week?" Otis asked, checking the patient's pulse.

"He is in shock! Put him on this operating table." Otis continued, giving orders to the guards.

The guards obeyed, carefully placing the prisoner on the table. As Otis examined the man, his heart sank at the sight of the bite marks on the prisoner's arms and face, evidence of the relentless rat attack. Additionally, the disfigurement of his legs from the broken kneecaps and the apparently busted eardrum highlighted the brutal nature of the warden's actions.

"Doctor! Nurse! Please get over here!" Otis yelled out at the start, calling someone to attend the patient.

As the doctor's urgent voice resonated through the medical ward, the guards swiftly carried the injured prisoner to the operating table and gently laid him on his back. Otis's experienced eyes quickly assessed the extent of the prisoner's injuries. The gruesome scene before him revealed the devastating aftermath of the rat attack.

"What happened to him, Dr. Bush?" The nurse asked the doctor. She was pounding as she came running.

"Put this man to sleep before he dies from shock and give him a full examination. Check out his skull—I won't be surprised if it's fractured." Otis said.

The nurse quickly prepared the necessary sedative and administered it to the injured prisoner. Within moments, his groans of pain subsided as he slipped into a deep sleep.

As Otis examined the prisoner, he carefully assessed the extent of the injuries caused by the rats' bites and the vicious beating. The doctor's expression turned grave as he observed the deep wounds on the man's arms and face.

"My skull feels like it's been separated from my brain," mumbled the unconscious prisoner.

Otis turned his attention to the disfigurement of the prisoner's legs, caused by the brutal blows to his kneecaps. He shook his head in disbelief and anger."Who did this?" he asked, his voice filled with frustration.

"The warden or governor, whatever you want to call him," replied the other prisoner who had witnessed the horrific ordeal.

Otis turned to the guards who had brought in the injured prisoners. "How could you let this happen?" he demanded, his anger evident in his tone.

"We were just following orders," one of the guards responded, avoiding eye contact.

Meanwhile, the nurse had come back with a cast and started carefully applying it to the injured man's broken wrist and hand.

"I knew this was going to happen," Otis muttered to himself, shaking his head in dismay. He called out to the nurse, "Come here and put a cast on this man's wrist and hand. I'll be right back. I'm going to go talk to the warden."

With that, Otis hurriedly left the medical ward, determined to confront the warden about the appalling treatment of the prisoners. As he made his way through the prison, his mind swirled with anger and concern for the well-being of the inmates under the warden's control. The nurse takes the prisoner with her. Otis and the guards leave.

XIII

Inside the prison, in Jack's office, Jack has on a suit and is sitting behind his new fancy desk with gold trim. He's talking on the phone, which is gold too.

"How are we looking at ticket sales for tonight's event?" Jack asked Carl.

"We have 2,000 seats, and they're sold out," Carl replied.

Jack's face lit up with satisfaction at the news. "Good! That's a quick $50,000. Hold on for a minute Carl. David's voice came through the intercom, "Yes, Sir."

"Come to my office and bring the list with you," Jack commanded.

"I'll be right there," David replied promptly.

As Jack released the hold button, he leaned back in his chair, a smug expression crossing his face. The excitement of the sold-out event and the prospect of making a quick $50,000 seemed to invigorate him.

Within moments, David entered the office, carrying a folder in his hands.

"Here is the list that you wanted, Sir," David said, extending the folder to Jack.

Taking the folder, Jack looked through its contents. "Good. These are all the names of the prisoners we're going to execute tonight?" he confirmed.

David nodded, "That's right, Sir. Their nicknames are underneath their real names. The families who are coming and want to push the buttons themselves are right beside the prisoners' names."

Jack's eyes scanned the list, his mind calculating the possibilities.

"I'm surprised that more of the victims' families don't want to be present. I only see five out of fifteen," Jack remarked.

David explained, "Oh no, Sir, they're all here, but I just gave you a list of the ones that want to press the button themselves."

"Ah, I see now. Good job, David," Jack acknowledged with a nod. "That'll be all. See you tonight."

Before David could leave, another concern crossed Jack's mind.

"Oh, by the way, make sure all of the prisoners who are going to be executed have on gym shorts and nothing else. And make sure they are tied up with rope and tape because we can't put metal in the microwave," Jack instructed.

"Will do, Sir," David replied, heading for the door.

As David left, Jack settled back into his chair. His mind focused on the impending event. Little did he know that the brutal decisions he made would come back to haunt him.

The prison auditorium is filled with spectators, and half of them are a little drunk and making noise. The TV people are ready and doing last minutes checks. Jack is on stage. He's wearing a suit and carrying his stick. Jack walks over to the family members that are there to press the button. They're seated on the right side of the microwave, and it's covered up. Jack is shaking their hands one by one. A victim's family member stands up and gives Jack a hug when he goes to shake her hand.

As the audience watched the horrifying spectacle, the atmosphere in the auditorium was a mix of excitement and fear. Some spectators expressed shock and disgust at the gruesome sight before them.

"I had no idea it was going to be this gross," a Woman in the audience said; she was repulsed by the graphic display.

The man sitting next to her chimed in, "I'll tell you what! After seeing this, I'll never commit murder, rape, or anything else that will get me inside that microwave."

"You got that shit right!" agreed the man next to him.

Meanwhile, the guards, including David and Jerry, were struggling to control the restive inmates who were going crazy witnessing their fellow prisoner's brutal execution.

"You may as well sit down and take it like a man," Jack taunted them, reveling in their distress, talking to his inmates.

Suddenly, the microwave sprinkler system activated, and Jack proceeded to retrieve the remains, showing the crushed bones to the audience.

"Here is $25,000 of the taxpayers' money we don't have to worry about anymore," he declared triumphantly, further fueling the crowd's cheering.

As Jack continued with the executions, his sadistic amusement grew, and he taunted the inmates with callous remarks, which only fueled their restlessness.

In another part of St. Louis, inside a house, a violent altercation ensued between a man and a woman. Their fight was momentarily interrupted when Jack's face appeared on the TV screen, announcing the next execution.

"MAN, I'm gonna kill you right now," the man threatened, brandishing a knife.

But as they watched Pinhead's horrifying demise on TV, the couple's attention was diverted, and they were both captivated by the gruesome spectacle unfolding.

As the rapist attacked another woman in her home, he was startled to witness Pinhead's fate on television.

"RAPIST Hey! You're not Sally. I'm in the wrong house," he stammered, realizing his mistake.

However, the woman was not easily swayed, threatening him with the same fate as the executed inmates.

"You're lying. I'm going to have your ass tossed into that microwave," she declared, determined to defend herself.

In an attempt to escape his impending doom, the rapist offered her money as an apology, hoping it would dissuade her from carrying out her threat.

"Look! It's a big misunderstanding. To show you how sorry I am, here is 500 dollars," he pleaded, desperately trying to avoid a gruesome fate.

As the televised executions continued, Jack's reign of terror cast a dark shadow over Missouri, leaving the prisoners and the general public alike in a state of dread and uncertainty. Little did they know that these brutal decisions would come back to haunt Jack and everyone involved in this macabre event.

The rapist, terrified and desperate to escape the fate he witnessed on TV, runs out of the house, leaving the relieved woman behind.

"Thank God! Thank you, Governor Jack Blake," Woman 2 exclaims gratefully.

Inside Mutt Dog and Hen J's prison cell, they watch Jack on TV, discussing the ongoing executions.

"I knew it, I knew it. The nigga done came out in him," Mutt Dog remarks, sensing the sadistic side of Jack's personality.

"One day, my brother Reggie is going to be in that thing. We're going to have to do something," Hen J says worriedly.

"Do what? He's only the warden and the governor, so what can you do? I'll tell you what you can do; go along with the program because if you don't, you just might find your ass in that microwave," Mutt Dog warns, emphasizing the grim consequences of defying Jack's rule.

In Kansas City, inside a gas station, Jack's face appears on the TV while three men walk in, intending to rob the place. Oblivious to the danger, the gas station employee is fixated on the TV.

"Okay, this is a hold-up! Don't move, or I will kill your ass!" the second man threatens, brandishing a gun.

The third man goes behind the counter and opens the cash register to take the money.

Just then, the TV broadcast captures their attention when they hear Jack mention the next execution, Lance Jones, also known as Microwave.

"Hey! Did I hear someone say Lance Jones?" the man at the door questions.

"You talking about Microwave? He's in the house on death row," the third man confirms.

"Is this you guys' buddy? Because if it is, they're getting ready to kill him?" the gas station employee informs them, still focused on the TV.

"Damn! That does look like Microwave," the second man observes, realizing the gravity of the situation.

As everyone's attention is fixed on the TV, Jack continues with his commentary.

"Hey, you'll never believe what his nickname is. Out of all things, they call him Microwave. Well, the Microwave is going into the microwave, and here is the woman that Microwave left a widower. She's here to set the timer and press the button herself."

Back at the prison, David and Jerry bring Microwave, who is sobbing, up to the microwave. The gravity of the situation dawns on Microwave, and he realizes the horrifying fate that awaits him.

"Die, you fucker! Die! You killed my husband! Die!" The widow screamed.

The microwave starts shaking, and his eyes are bleeding. His chest splits down the middle and blood pours out. His eyes pop so far out that they hit the glass and rolled into the back of the microwave.

While the men were engrossed in the content on the TV, an unexpected event occurred. Suddenly, the microwave burst into a violent explosion, disrupting the calm of the scene. Startled, the three robbers jolted back in unison, their attention abruptly torn away from the television screen. Jack and the widow jumped up and down, giving each other high fives.

In the gas station, the group of men exchanged puzzled glances, their attention now diverted from their previous activities to the TV screen. They watched in disbelief as the news report showed Jack, standing amidst the aftermath of the microwave explosion, holding its damaged remains.

Jack's confident remark, "Three down and twelve to go!" added an air of excitement and mystery to the unfolding events.

The men in the gas station were left intrigued, trying to decipher the significance of Jack's words and actions. The room filled with a mix of anticipation and uncertainty, as they now realized they were dealing with someone determined and formidable. The scene set the stage for a thrilling encounter, leaving the audience eager to see how the rest of the story would unfold and what challenges awaited the robbers and Jack in their high-stakes pursuit.

As the third man puts the money back, clearly disheartened and frustrated, he exclaims, "Fuck this! I'm gonna get my job back at McDonald's!" He storms out of the door, abandoning their ill-fated robbery attempt.

The second man, still gripping the gun, is left visibly shaken and anxious. He calls out to someone named Dre, seeking reassurance and support in the tense situation.

The employee calmly interjects, "If Dre was the one standing by the door, he left before the other one did." The revelation adds to the confusion in the room, leaving the second man uncertain and isolated in his predicament.

The scene captures the unraveling of the robbery, with emotions running high and the plan falling apart. The uncertainty of Dre's whereabouts further intensifies the situation, leaving the audience wondering about the outcome and the consequences the remaining robber might face.

As the second man, clearly overwhelmed by fear and guilt, hands over the gun with shaky hands, he pleads, "Here! Take the gun. I don't want it. I was never here, okay?" He hurriedly places the gun on the counter before making a hasty escape from the gas station, desperate to distance himself from the failed robbery.

The relieved employee, amused by the absurdity of the situation, starts laughing to himself. He raises a bottle, hidden beneath the counter, and exclaims, "Jack, you're controlling crime already. You've got my vote next election!" He toasts to the TV, acknowledging the unseen presence of Jack, and takes a drink to celebrate the unexpected turn of events.

XIV

On stage, Jack is full of energy, bouncing around and hyping up the crowd. His movements take him to the far end of the stage, and both he and the guards are engrossed in the electric atmosphere, their attention straying from the death row inmates.

Taking the microphone, Jack announces, "Our next execution will be Alex Jimmerson, better known as XMan." His words send a wave of excitement through the crowd, the volume rising into a thunderous roar.

Suddenly, a shout from the crowd pierces the din, "They're getting away!" The words catch Jack's attention, jolting him out of his role as the entertainer. The scene ends on a cliffhanger, leaving the audience wondering about the escape attempt and what will happen next.

Jack looks over to the other end of the stage and sees that the death row inmates are not in their seats. They're on the floor. Somehow they organized themselves so they could be able to move together without falling over each other. The inmates looked like a caterpillar as they were trying to run since their feet were tied so close together, and they could only take little steps. When Jack sees that they're trying to get away, he becomes very angry.

"I've told you, dumb inmates, that the only place you all are going is in this microwave," Jack said angrily.

Jack grabs his stick and hops off the stage. He catches up with the inmates. X-Man's leading the pack. Jack walks in front of him and swings his stick very hard, and hits X-Man on his kneecap. Jack hits him so hard that his bone comes through his skin, but X-Man will not go down. He continues moving, hopping on one leg.

"I don't believe this shit," Jack replied, shaking his head.

Jack walks on the other side of X-Man. Jack swings viciously at his other leg and cracks the kneecap. X-Man falls to the floor, and some of the inmates fall on top of him while the others fall off to the side.

"David and Jerry! Come and get X-Man. Unhook him and throw him in the microwave." Jack shouted and called David and Jerry. They did just as Jack said. As they carried X-Man to the stage, he kept cursing Jack.

"You faggot motherfucker; you broke my kneecaps!" X-man screamed in pain.

Jack walked toward him and said, "Don't worry about it because in a few minutes the pain will be over."

X-man spits in Jack's face, leaving Jack furious. Jack comes over the top of his head with the stick and hits X-Man in the head. Splitting it wide open. Blood goes everywhere.

"Hurry up and get his ass in there. We're running out of time." Jack said. It felt like he was quite ruthless at that time.

David and Jerry put X-Man in the microwave, and Jack sets the timer and presses the button. There is scene after scene of Jack executing the inmates. Jack is constantly jumping up and down. He's giving the victims' family members high-fives, and after the executions, they are able to do it themselves. The last execution is over, and Jack walks back to the center of the stage.

As the tension-filled moment elevates, Jack raises his voice to address the crowd with a forced smile."Hey everybody! Wasn't that fun?" he exclaims

As the crowd erupts into cheers, Jack's confidence and charisma shine through. He seizes the opportunity to keep the positive momentum going and addresses the enthusiastic audience, "I will see you all back here next week. We'll execute fifteen more death row inmates. Thank you and goodbye."

His words are met with applause and excitement, reaffirming the anticipation for the next event. Jack's ability to command the crowd's attention and engage them leaves a lasting impression, ensuring that the upcoming gathering will be eagerly anticipated by all. The scene ends on a high note, leaving the audience looking forward to the next chapter of the story.

As Jack walks off the stage, he is greeted by Carl, who seems puzzled by the turn of events and says to him, "Jack, I thought you said that you were going to do this every day. You know, like the lottery."

Carl's confusion is evident as he questions Jack about his plans. Jack, perhaps realizing that he had promised something different, takes a moment to respond.

"Well, you see, Carl, things got a bit complicated today. But don't worry, we'll figure it out. Tomorrow's another day." Jack replied with a sheepish smile.

Jack's reassurance leaves Carl slightly relieved, knowing that Jack will find a solution to the situation. The camaraderie between the two suggests a strong bond and understanding, leaving the audience curious about how they will tackle the challenges that lie ahead.

As Jack explains his change of plans to Carl, the atmosphere between them is one of camaraderie and mutual understanding.

"I was going to, but I thought about it, and we could get more money out of the TV stations by doing it once a week. And I don't want people getting tired of it. Besides, I want to give them something to look forward to. I don't really have the time every day either." Jack continues

Carl nods, acknowledging Jack's reasoning and decision-making process. "You are the boss."

A gesture of approval and camaraderie, Jack pats Carl on the back. The two friends walk away together, ready to face whatever challenges and adventures await them in the days to come. The scene ends on a note of respect and understanding between Jack and Carl, leaving the audience with a sense of companionship and anticipation for their future endeavors.

The next day inside Jack's office at the prison, Jack sits behind his desk, intently reviewing a stack of papers. Suddenly, a soft knock on the door disrupts his concentration.

"Come in," Jack responds, lifting his gaze from the documents.

In strides David and Jerry, their faces reflecting a sense of urgency and concern.

"Sir, something is going on that you need to know about," David informs Jack, his voice serious.

Jack leans forward, intrigued by the gravity of their words. "What is it?" he asks, his curiosity evident.

The scene is set for a crucial revelation, and the audience is left eager to discover the news that has drawn David and Jerry to seek Jack's attention. The air in the room crackles with tension, hinting at the potential impact of this unfolding event on the prison's affairs and Jack's role as the warden.

The atmosphere in Jack's office became tense as Jerry delivered the troubling news. "The prisoners are really upset about the executions last night, and they're planning a riot," he revealed, his concern evident.

Jack leaned back in his chair, unfazed by the revelation. "That doesn't surprise me. As a matter of fact, I expected something like this to happen, so I came up with a plan," Jack calmly replied, his confidence shining through.

Jerry's curiosity was piqued, and he leaned in, eager to hear Jack's strategy. "Oh really! What do you have in mind?" he inquired.

A faint smile crossed Jack's face as he divulged his plan. "I want you and David to round up all the prisoners with the most influence and bring them to my office immediately. Try to do this without letting the other prisoners know," he explained, emphasizing the need for secrecy.

One hour had passed since Jack had requested Jerry and David to gather the prisoners with the most influence. Now, inside Jack's office, a formidable group stood before him, including Mutt Dog, Hen J, Deliverance, Executioner, Row-Bo, Big Ed, Abdul (a Muslim), and Razor. The atmosphere in the room was charged with tension as all eyes were fixed on Jack, seated behind his desk with his stick prominently displayed.

Getting straight to the point, Jack addressed the prisoners, acknowledging their discontent with his method of execution and the rumored plans for a riot. "What I want from you gentlemen is to make sure that it doesn't happen since you have the most influence over the inmates," Jack emphasized, his voice firm but composed.

Razor, known for his defiance, attempted to play it off, responding, "I don't know what in the hell you're talking about."

Undeterred by Razor's response, Jack's tone escalated, showing his unwavering determination. "Don't play with me. You know damn well what I'm talking about," he retorted, making it clear that he was aware of the brewing unrest among the prisoners.

Inside Jack's office, the tension remained palpable as the influential prisoners engaged in a confrontation with Jack. The Executioner, known for his no-nonsense demeanor, challenged Jack's request for their assistance in averting a potential riot.

"I'm not saying that we're planning a riot, but if we were, why should we help you?" the Executioner questioned, his voice steely.

With a hint of persuasion, Jack responded, "Because I'm going to make all of you a deal of a lifetime, and I do mean lifetime, considering that is what you all have anyway. The only difference is that none of you are on death row, and the couple of guys in here that don't have life, well, by the time they get out, their life will be almost over anyway."

Abdul, cautious and protective of his Muslim brothers, remained skeptical. "So, why should I trust you and turn my back on my Muslim brothers?" he inquired.

"I'll keep my word. A real man keeps his word, and I promise that I'll execute death row inmates, and I'm doing it!" Jack declared firmly. He continued, "Besides Abdul,

I looked at your file, and you were not a Muslim when you came in here. You joined for protection, but now you've moved up, and I want you to use your influence to keep your group of people in check, and that goes for all of you."

The prisoners were still curious about the "lifetime deal" Jack mentioned earlier. Row-Bo spoke up, asking, "So what is this lifetime deal?"

Jack leaned forward, revealing his proposal. "All of you men will walk out of here one year from today's date. And, I'll give each one of you $25,000. So do we have a deal?" he proposed, seeking their agreement.

Hen J whispered to Mutt Dog, "If I decide to go along with your plan, I want to know if I can exchange my $25,000 for my brother Reggie, who's now on death row, and he walks out of here with us?"

"I don't see a problem with that," Mutt Dog replied.

Jack overheard their conversation and said, "Well, I guess you're going to have to take your chances."

Mutt Dog gave Jack a mean look, but before they could discuss further, Row-Bo chimed in, "Well, you know it's like um-um, well you know what I am saying?"

Jack looked puzzled by Row-Bo's response and glanced at David and Jerry.

"I thought I told you two to bring me the prisoners with the most influence," Jack said in frustration.

"We did," Jerry replied.

"You couldn't have. Hell, this guy can't even talk, and if he is one of the ringleaders around here, it's no wonder why we're dealing with a bunch of bozos," Jack retorted.

Big Ed added, "What he's trying to say is, how do we know that we can trust you? What if some of us want to, but a few of us don't? The word will get around, and whoever takes your side is in for a whole lot of trouble from the other inmates."

"I expected all of you to go along with this. What's the problem? You all will be out in one year, and I'm giving each one of you $25,000. What in the hell else can you ask for?" Jack said, growing impatient.

Abdul hesitated, "I don't know if I can do this."

"Me either," Razor added.

"Wait a minute. Are you two stupid sons-of-a-bitches trying to tell me that you're willing to throw away a chance at freedom and money because you're loyal to a bunch of losers that really don't give a damn about you in the first place? Hell, you clowns are crazier than I thought," Jack exclaimed, frustration mounting.

Deliverance said, "Well, I'm not crazy. I'll go along with you. One year sounds a hell of a lot better than fifty."

"Count me in," the Executioner chimed in.

"That's two. What about the rest of you?" Jack asked.

Executioner and Deliverance stood off to the side of the other inmates next to Jerry and David.

The prisoners exchanged nervous glances, unsure of how to proceed.

"Hell with this. If me and my brother can go free after one year, I'm with you, Warden," Hen J declared, walking over to where Executioner and Deliverance were standing.

"I'm in," Big Ed said, following Hen J.

Row-Bo, still not making any sense, nodded his head in agreement.

Jack interrupted him, "Look here! Just nod your head yes or no, and please don't try to talk."

Row-Bo nodded his head yes and walked over to where the others were standing.

Jack turned his attention to the remaining prisoners, "So, what have you all decided?"

Mutt Dog asked cautiously, "Do you promise to keep your word?"

"I promise," Jack replied.

"Hen J is right. We came in here together; let's walk out of here together. We don't have anything to lose, plus he's going to give us $25,000. Don't be a fool," Mutt Dog urged.

"Better than that. I'll give you all $50,000 each. So, Hen J, that means you get your brother out and $25,000!" Jack declared, trying to sway Mutt Dog.

After some hesitation, Mutt Dog finally said, "Okay, I'm in."

Jack then turned to Razor and Abdul, "Well, that leaves you two. So, what's it going to be?"

The tension in the room was palpable as Abdul and Razor exchanged glances.

"So, what will happen if we decide not to do this?" Abdul asked.

"I'll kill you on the spot, right now, and pull the next ranked man behind you, and I'll keep pulling until I find someone who will go along with the program," Jack threatened.

"I'm in. I know if I don't take it, somebody else will," Abdul reluctantly agreed.

Razor, however, remained firm in his resistance, declaring, "I'm not selling out to this shit. You're gonna have to kill me."

The tense standoff continued, with Razor standing his ground against Jack's offer.

❧

Jack reached into one of his drawers behind the desk and pulled out a gun. He got up out of his seat and walked over to Razor, pointing the gun at his head. Razor showed no emotion.

"Last chance!" Jack warned.

"I am not selling out!" Razor replied firmly.

See ya!

Jack pulled the trigger, and Razor's brains splattered all over the floor.

"Dumb ass! David, bring the next man in here ranked right behind Razor," Jack ordered.

"Yes, Sir," David acknowledged and left the room.

"Do any of you all have a problem with what I just did?" Jack inquired.

"Hell no! If he's not with us, then he's against us!" Deliverance chimed in.

"What about the rest of you?" Jack asked, and the prisoners shook their heads, indicating that they didn't have a problem with what he did.

"Now, let's get something straight- I don't want no riots, not one! Because if there is one uprising in here, the deal is off! I'll kill every last one of you sons of bitches, just like I just did with this piece of shit lying here!" Jack's tone grew stern.

David returned to Jack's office with the prisoner ranked next to Razor, Dyno.

"What the hell did you do to him? You motherfucker!" Dyno charged at Jack but was restrained by the guards and a few prisoners. He was upset.

"Listen to what the warden has to say," Executioner advised, and Dyno calmed down.

"I offered the men $50,000 and one more year in jail to keep a riot from happening. They all agreed except Razor, and you see what happened to him. Now, I'm offering you the same thing since you're next in rank," Jack explained.

"Wait a minute. Are you telling me that you offered him $50,000 and one more year in jail, and he didn't take it? All he had to do was keep a riot from happening?" Dyno clarified.

"That's right," Jack confirmed.

"Now you're offering that same deal to me?" Dyno asked again.

"That's right," Jack nodded.

(Talking to the other prisoners)"Is he on the up and up?" Dyno inquired.

"You see us in here, don't you?" Big Ed responded.

(Smiling a little) "That means I will do one year instead of 35 years! And I get to be with my wife and kids and walk out of here with $50,000. Hell, I don't have to think twice about that," Dyno decided, his voice tinged with regret. "I don't know if you can hear me or not, Razor, but man, I'm sorry. I can't turn this down, and I can't believe that you did."

"Now that we have an understanding, before you men leave, I want you all to clean up my office. Get rid of this piece of shit!" Jack instructed.

"How am I going to explain what has happened to Razor to the other brothers?" Dyno asked, concerned.

"Tell them he has been transferred to an out-of-state prison, and you don't know which one," Jack suggested.

"Well, Sir, what do you want us to do with the body? Bury him?" Jerry asked.

"No! I don't want any evidence left. Put him in a body bag, and when the prisoners are asleep, take him into the kitchen and throw him into the grinder. We'll lose him like that. After all, it's not the first time it's been done," Jack said, laughing.

(Talking to the prisoners) "Oh, by the way fellas, you may want to skip dinner tomorrow because this is what you'll be having," Jack pointed to Razor.

As David and Jerry helped Razor back on his feet, the camera focused on the ring glinting on Razor's finger, hinting at its significance.

XV

The following day at dinner time, inside the prison cafe, the room was filled with prisoners enjoying their meals. Two inmates sat down at a table, setting their trays down. On their plates was meatloaf, a staple of the prison menu. With a few hungry bites, they began their meal, engaging in quiet conversation as they ate.

"Damn! This meatloaf is pretty good today," Prisoner 3 commented.

"I'm hip; every now and then, it tastes like this," Prisoner 4 agreed.

"Well, they need to fix it like this all the time," Prisoner 3 remarked.

(Prisoner 4 took another bite and crunch down on something.)

"What the hell is this?" Prisoner 3 asked.

He pulled the ring that belonged to Razor out of his mouth.

"Look, man! There was a ring in my meatloaf," Prisoner 3 exclaimed.

"No shit! Let me look through my meatloaf and see if I can find one," Prisoner 4 said.

"I bet one of those kitchen workers lost it off his hand while he was making the meatloaf," Prisoner 3 speculated.

"Well, put it into your pocket before somebody sees it. Maybe you can get some smokes for it," Prisoner 4 suggested.

"No, I like it too much to trade it off. I'm going to wait a while and wear it myself," Prisoner 1 replied.

INSIDE GOVERNOR'S MANSION: JACK'S BEDROOM- 12:00 NOON:

Jack was laying in bed asleep with three naked women. The women were asleep too. There was an empty liquor bottle and a couple of marijuana cigarettes next to the bottle. The telephone rang five times before Jack heard it. Jack was half awake and answered the phone.

"Hello!" Jack said.

"Jack, it's Carl. Did you forget that you were supposed to meet with the TV executives this afternoon?" Carl's voice came through the phone.

"Yes, I did. What time is the meeting?" Jack asked.

"Now! Are you okay, Jack? You don't sound too good," Carl inquired.

"No! I'm not feeling good at all," Jack replied.

"So! What do you want me to tell the TV executives, that you're under the weather and you would like to reschedule for another day?" Carl asked.

"No! Don't tell them that. Time will not permit it. How about if you make the deal," Jack suggested.

"Well, what should I do?" Carl asked.

"Take the highest offer," Jack said.

"Okay, I'll do my best. Talk to you later," Carl said before hanging up.

Jack hung up the phone and fell back to sleep.

❧

INSIDE JACK'S OFFICE- GOVERNORS MANSION- THE NEXT DAY:

Next day, in Governer's mansion, Carl walked in Jack's officer. He sees Jack was sitting at his desk, filling out some papers. He looked up and saw Carl.

"Just the man I want to see. Well, how did we do?" Jack asked eagerly.

"We're going to be dealing with Harry Fishburn and KKOT again for 25 million on a one-year's contract," Carl replied.

Jack's face contorted with a mix of surprise and frustration.

"All you were able to get was 25 million? I talked them out of 10 million for the first event. Well, I didn't talk them out of it, they just bided that high," Jack lamented.

"What did you start the bidding at?" Carl inquired.

"I didn't, I just let them outbid each other," Jack explained.

"I didn't know that was how you did it because I started the bidding at 20 million, and none of them would go any higher than 25. So that's what I took," Carl said, feeling unsure.

Jack shook his head with his hands over his face, clearly disappointed.

(Emotional) "I'm sorry Jack if I did something wrong?" Carl asked with concern.

(Waving his hands in the air) "No! You did nothing wrong. It's my fault. I should've been there instead of having a good time last night. Then I would have been able to get up and take care of business. Believe me, it won't happen again," Jack reassured.

"I'm just wondering, what did I do that was so obvious that they took advantage of me?" Carl pondered.

"Never start off the bidding with a high amount unless you know you're going to get it. They plan just like we do, and when I didn't show up for the meeting, that was right up their alley. When you said that they were bidding 20 million to start, they knew they didn't have to go much higher than that to satisfy your asking price!" Jack explained.

(Shaking his head) "I'm sorry, I just didn't know. I thought if they would pay 10 million, I could start off the bid at 20 million, and it would go up to 100 million," Carl defended his approach.

"I understand your way of thinking, but so did they. I have the rating reports on the event, and just about everyone in Missouri tuned in for it, but if I would have been there, like I should've, I could have used the rating reports to get more money. Hell, we're the only one doing this, not just in the nation, but all over the world. The sponsors are knocking down KKOT doors and giving them whatever they want for this because people all over the world want to see this. The other stations that were involved will probably get a kickback worth more than what we signed the contract for because they didn't try to outbid so hard," Jack explained.

"I really feel bad about this," Carl admitted.

"Don't feel bad because it is my fault, and I already have a plan to make up the differences," Jack reassured.

"Oh yeah! What's that?" Carl asked curiously.

"What we're doing is local right now, but it's going to go nationwide, maybe even worldwide. All we have to do is make sure we have enough prisoners on death row," Jack revealed.

"How are we going to do that?" Carl asked, intrigued.

"We're going to consolidate all of the prisoners into one prison within a year's time," Jack explained.

(Shocked) "How in the hell are you going to do that? The prisons are already overcrowded. That's why they were built in the first place," Carl questioned.

"They won't be when we let them all go," Jack said with a smirk.

"What! Are you crazy? If you do that, do you know how much hell is going to be going on out there in those streets?" Carl expressed concern.

(Smiling) "That's what I'm counting on," Jack replied.

(Shaking his head in disbelief) "I don't understand, Jack. After what happened to your family, I thought you would do anything possible to keep crime from happening," Carl said, disappointed.

"At first, that was the way I felt, but I didn't realize how much money could be made. I can't bring my family back, so I must get as much out of it as I can," Jack explained, his motives laid bare.

"Okay! Okay! I understand that, but tell me how are you going to let all of these prisoners go without anyone questioning your decision," Carl pressed.

"I'm going to let them go in large amounts every two months, where it won't really be noticeable. By the end of the year, five prisons will be closed. I will make a press statement that I have saved the Missouri taxpayers 750 million dollars when, in reality, I would have saved one billion dollars. That's what you and I will profit from, and I will give the Missouri people a kickback. I'll tell them that they do NOT have to pay for their license plates that year. They'll think, hey this guy is really for the people, not realizing that they're still paying taxes and the plates are paid for anyway with their tax dollars! We just decided to do something else with the money, like pocket a couple of million for ourselves!" Jack explained his devious plan.

"It sounds good, but do you think that the people will go for it?" Carl asked skeptically.

"Oh, hell yes! Remember one thing, everyone sells out cheap. The ones that don't, we'll give them a little extra.

They'll shut their mouths too," Jack laughed, sharing his cunning strategy.

Carl and Jack both start laughing.

"So, when are we going to put this plan into action?" Carl asked.

"Next week, but make sure that the lifers and the other death row inmates are transferred over to M.S.P.," Jack instructed.

"Will do, Sir," Carl acknowledged.

XVI

Eleven months later, inside the Governor's Mansion in Jack's den, a different scene unfolds. Jack is seen seated in a chair, holding a bottle of liquor in one hand and smoking a joint in the other. The room is dimly lit, and a TV screen displays Jack being interviewed by a reporter.

On the TV, Jack looks somewhat different from his earlier self, perhaps reflecting the toll that his position has taken on him. As the interview proceeds, the camera captures Jack's demeanor and the effects of his lifestyle choices, emphasizing the weight of his responsibilities and the challenges he faces as the warden.

"Governor Blake, how does it make you feel that you have made Missouri one of the safest places in the nation to live by cutting the rape and murder rate by 98% and the overall crime rate by 75%?" the reporter asked on the TV.

The Keeper of the Castle

(Smiling) "Well, I promised that I was going to do something about it, and dog took it, I meant it!" Jack replied proudly.

"All of the people I talked to are so happy about not having to pay for his or her license plates this year, me included," the reporter added.

"Well, the people of Missouri deserve it. After all, McDonald's isn't going to be the only place where you're going to get a break today. I would love to talk to you more, but I have a meeting, and I'm already running late, so please excuse me," Jack said, smoothly excusing himself.

Jack walked off and hopped into his limousine.

"That is one hell of a guy. I don't mind saying it; he has my vote for re-election!" the reporter praised.

Inside Jack's office, the tense atmosphere is heightened as Jack's frustration reaches its peak. In a fit of anger, he hurls the bottle he was drinking from against the wall, the sound of shattering glass echoing in the room.

Just as Jack tries to regain his composure, a knock on the door startles him. Realizing he needs to hide any evidence of his indulgence, he quickly extinguishes the joint he was smoking and grabs an air freshener, spraying it in an attempt to mask the lingering scent.

With the room now seemingly presentable, Jack tries to compose himself before inviting the visitor in.

"Come in," he calls out, his voice masking the turmoil within him.

Carl walked through the door.

"Well, Jack, I think you out-thought yourself on this one. Since we passed the law ten months ago that rapists and child molesters will get the microwave, there have only been eleven rapes, fifteen child molestations, and seven murders in all of Missouri! We only have ninety death row inmates, and that's enough to finish out this year. One month into next year, we're done," Carl reported.

(Mad) "I can't believe that all of those prisoners I let go are actually staying out of trouble," Jack fumed.

"Yes, it's hard to believe, and the ones that have been taken back into custody have not been arrested for murder, rape, or child molestation. You have really put fear in the hearts and minds of the people of Missouri," Carl said, impressed.

Jack sat back in his chair and then jumped up, angrily slamming his hand on the desk.

"Damn! I was counting on that 100 million this year!" Jack vented his frustration.

"Well, we have 40 to start off the year with, but we would need 500 more people to commit murders, rapes, or child molestations to get the TV contract for the year. Everyone is so scared of going into that microwave that nobody is committing those types of crimes anymore," Carl explained.

"I just can't believe this shit," Jack grumbled.

"Well, Jack, maybe something else will come up that you will be able to take advantage of," Carl suggested.

"Advantage of what? Get the Senate to pass a law that we can throw shoplifters and J-walkers into the microwave. Hell, I just screwed up," Jack bemoaned.

"Well, I'm getting ready to leave. Call me if you need me, and, by the way, we'll be closing the last of the prisons tomorrow. The remaining death row inmates will be at M.S.P. before noon. See you later, Jack," Carl said, ready to depart.

Jack didn't say anything as Carl walked out the door. The TV was on in the background, and a news reporter was talking about current events. Jack stood in the middle of the floor in a daze, then he grabbed his stick and started swinging it at everything in sight. He broke a lamp, hit a glass picture on the wall, and walked over to the TV. He was getting ready to hit it until the newscaster said something that caught his attention.

(On TV) "That's right! I will repeat what I just said, and yes, it's true. A Japanese surgeon named Otto Yosoto has come up with a new method used to attach human body parts to other humans that have lost their limbs. So that means there is new hope for people who have lost their legs and arms due to accidents and for war veterans who lost their limbs while serving their country. The good news is for war veterans that lost their limbs while in combat, the government will pay for anyone that wants the operation. The bad news is, according to Mr. Yosoto, the donor has to be alive. They cannot be dead, not even for one minute, so you can imagine how many donors are going to come forward for this project. Frankly speaking, anyone that is alive is not going to be ready to donate his or her body parts to someone else. Yours truly is one of them, but I must give Mr. Yosoto his dues. A magnificent breakthrough in modern technology. Moving on to other news..." the newscaster reported.

Jack turned down the TV and started talking to himself.

(Smiling) "Don't give up so quickly, Mr. Yosoto, I got all of the donors you need!" Jack said with a sinister grin.

Jack rushed over to the phone and picked it up, dialing a number.

"Carl! This is Jack; I just figured out what we're going to do!"

※

Carl furrowed his brow, contemplating Jack's words. "Okay, but why do you want to do this? That means we would have to re-open some of the prisons we just closed," he said, seeking clarification.

"Trust me, this plan will be self-sustaining," Jack replied confidently. "I'll explain it all in detail tomorrow. Oh, and there's one more thing I need you to take care of."

Curiosity piqued, Carl asked, "Sure, Jack. What is it?"

"Please contact channel 5 news and inquire about how we can get in touch with a Japanese surgeon named Mr. Yosoto. Once you learn about his abilities, everything will become clearer to you. See you tomorrow," Jack instructed.

With that, Jack hung up the phone and couldn't contain his excitement, jumping around and yelling in anticipation.

The following day, Jack and Carl emerged from the Senate House together. The weight of the impending decision seemed to linger in the air.

"I can hardly believe they're going to pass that bill into law," Carl remarked, still processing the gravity of the situation.

"Why not? I can," Jack replied with a hint of pride. "First of all, each senator will receive $25,000. Secondly, some of those senators have family members who have suffered the loss of limbs due to cancer, accidents, or other reasons. For instance, Bill Cone's wife lost both of her legs. You can imagine how thrilled he'll be to know she can walk again, perhaps even with better prosthetics."

Carl chuckled at the thought. "Yeah, almost seems like they did her a favor."

As they made their way to their waiting limousines, Jack shared his plans. "I'm heading to M.S.P. to take on the role of warden. Call me at my office once you've gathered more information about Mr. Yosoto."

"I called them yesterday, and they assured me the information would be ready today. I'm heading to the TV station now. See you later," Carl confirmed.

Jack and Carl parted ways, both knowing that the road ahead would be filled with challenges and uncertainties. The fate of countless prisoners and the implications of the new law weighed heavily on their minds as they drove off to fulfill their respective roles.

"Yeah, you're right! It's them," Prisoner 2 chimed in, squinting his eyes to get a better look.

The other prisoners around them started whispering and murmuring, their attention now fully on K-9 and Da-Bo. These two inmates had gained a fearsome reputation in the prison for their violent tendencies and merciless ways.

Prisoner 1 spoke again, his voice filled with bitterness, "It's because of them that we're going through so much hell now. Microwave or no microwave, if I get the chance, I'm going to do something scary!"

Prisoner 2 chuckled darkly, "Hell, if you do that, the warden may give you a pardon just to get rid of K-9 and Da-Bo!"

The grim humor spread among the prisoners, but deep down, they all knew the truth. Crossing paths with K-9 and Da-Bo was like tempting fate, and no one dared to challenge them directly.

Meanwhile, inside his office, Jack stood by the window, watching the prisoners getting off the bus. He was dressed in his intimidating fatigues, tightly gripping his baton, his face contorted with malice.

"Yes! Yes! I have been waiting for you clowns for a while," he muttered to himself. "I am going to make your lives a living hell."

Back in the prison hallway, Jack and his guards continued their rounds. As they walked, they passed by a restroom where the muffled sounds of distress caught Jack's attention.

"Please! Don't!" a desperate voice pleaded.

"Shut up!" another voice barked harshly.

Jack stopped in his tracks, turning towards the restroom. The sinister grin on his face widened as he recognized the voices. The unfortunate soul inside was about to experience the wrath of K-9 and Da-Bo.

Without a hint of compassion, Jack motioned for his guards to follow him as he headed towards the source of the commotion. His sadistic intentions were clear, and the other prisoners knew better than to interfere.

Inside the prison walls, a dangerous power play was about to unfold, leaving the inmates to grapple with their worst nightmares.

※

Jack and the guards rush in and see eight men about to rape a young boy that is about eighteen years old. The other prisoners are holding the boy down while another is ripping off his clothes. None of them have noticed Jack.

"I hope that all of you know that rapists gets the microwave!" Jack said, He wanted them to pay for their crimes once and for all.

The prisoners stopped what they were doing. Everyone, including the boy, looked at Jack in surprise.

"Well, damn warden, I'm tired of jacking-off!" One of the prisoners said.

"Why should you be tired of what you really are?" Jack asked giving him a grave look. "I have someone else in mind for you. Let the boy go and follow me." He continued.

The prisoners released the boy and obediently followed Jack. Jack swiftly pulled out his walkie-talkie and called for Jerry.

"Come in, Jerry! Over!" Jack's voice echoed through the walkie-talkie.

"I'm here, Sir," Jerry responded promptly.

"Jerry, I want you to bring Lincoln Jones and Francis Johnson to cellblock O waiting room," Jack commanded. "Make sure that they are wearing those special uniforms I ordered for rapists and child molesters. If they put up a fight, hit them with the stun gun and dress them up in their new uniforms yourself."

Jerry acknowledged, "Will do, Sir! Over!"

XVII

Inside Cellblock O waiting room, Jerry stood by the door with the other guards surrounding him. There was a knock on the door, and Jerry opened it to find Jack standing in the doorway. Jack walked in, followed by the guards and the other prisoners. The camera angle shifted to Da-Bo and K-9, who were tied up in chairs. They were dressed in pink dresses with matching bonnets adorned with white ruffles. Both Da-Bo and K-9 appeared disoriented from the effects of the stun gun, but they were slowly regaining awareness. As of now, they hadn't noticed Jack's presence as their heads remained lowered, facing the floor.

Jack sneered, "My, my, my, don't we look real nice and pretty today. HA! HA!"

Da-Bo and K-9 looked up, their faces showing a mix of confusion and anger upon hearing Jack's voice.

Jerry chimed in, "They may be a little out of it, Sir. We had hell trying to get them into these dresses. We must have hit them with the stun gun 8 or 9 times before they were immobilized."

Jack grinned, looking at K-9 and Da-Bo with a twisted sense of satisfaction. "Good job, Jerry. Do you guys have any idea how long I've been waiting for this moment? I bet you all thought I forgot about you two. Well, I have some good news and some bad news. The good news is that even though you're both murderers and rapists, I'm not going to put you in the microwave. But the bad news is that once I'm finished with you, you're going to wish that I had."

K-9 asked nervously, "So, what do you plan on doing?"

Jack's eyes darted to the other prisoners, a sinister smile on his face. "It's not what I'm going to do; it's what they're going to do!" he said, pointing at the other inmates. "They're going to rape you two punks, just like you all did to my wife. But in your case, it's not going to be a one-time thing, oh no! You all are going to look forward to this every day. Hell, maybe even three or four times a day, so you better get used to it."

K-9 protested, "To hell with that! I've never been gang-raped!"

DA-BO added with fear in his voice, "I've only been gang-raped once, and I promised myself it would never happen again!"

Jack laughed mockingly, relishing their vulnerability. "Well, girls, never say never. HA! HA!" he taunted. Turning to the other prisoners, he commanded, "Okay, fellas! Do what you want with them."

The prisoners advanced menacingly toward K-9 and Da-Bo, their faces contorted with malice.

"I never liked you anyway K-9. Give me a blowjob!" Prisoner 1 said, giving a sick look to K9.

OVER THE SHOULDER ANGLE:

The prisoner is standing in front of K-9. He unzips his pants, however K9 moves his head away, trying avoid his sex organ.

"Come on and suck it, you punk!" The prisoner yelled.

❦

Prisoner 1 struck K-9 forcefully on the head, causing K-9 to lower his head in response.

Prisoner#1 suddenly lets out a piercing scream, his back turned to the scene. He slowly turns around, desperately covering himself with his hands, and tears streaming down his face. Jack stares at him with a mix of disbelief and contempt, unable to fathom the prisoner's reaction.

Jack scolded, "What the hell is wrong with you!"

Prisoner 1 cried out, "He bit me real hard!"

Jack looks at K-9 hard and K-9 is looking back at Jack the same way.

"So you don't want to do this? After what you did to my wife and family, you don't think you're not going to do this?" Jack questioned him.

K-9 retorted, "Hell naw!"

Jack replied, "Well, we'll just see about that!"

Jack walked over to K-9, locking eyes with him. He then turned his back and took a couple of steps forward before swiftly turning back around, swinging his stick with brutal force, and striking K-9 in the mouth. Half of K-9's teeth went flying out, and blood poured down his chin, leaving him in agonizing pain.

Addressing the other prisoners, Jack taunted, "Well, you all won't have any problem out of him now. Not only does he not have teeth to bite with, but I think I broke his jaw, so he can't apply any pressure either. HA! HA!"

Turning his attention to Da-Bo, Jack asked, "Do you have a problem with this?"

Da-Bo looked straight into Jack's eyes and said, "Man, you may as well kill me now because I'm not going to be going through this shit. I'll kill myself first."

"Oh no you won't because you won't be able to," Jack confidently replied.

"How do you figure that?" Da-Bo inquired, seeking an explanation.

"Because first, I am going to break both of your arms," Jack declared.

Jack swung his stick with force, hitting Da-Bo's arms, and the sound of bones breaking echoed in the room. Da-Bo let out agonizing screams as the pain overwhelmed him. Without hesitation, Jack delivered the same brutal blow to Da-Bo's other arm, causing him even more excruciating pain.

"Now, I would like to see how you're going to kill yourself? You can't use your arms or legs."

He then turned to K-9 and said, "Don't think that you're getting off that easy!"

As Da-Bo writhed in pain, Jack turned his attention to K-9, making it clear that he wouldn't let him escape the torment either.

K-9 is looking up at Jack and Jack does the same thing to him that he just did to Da-Bo. Now both men are screaming.

※

"Don't think I feel sorry for any of you monsters! Were my wife and kids screaming and crying like you two fools are now, before you killed them?" Jack yelled furiously.

His voice reverberated through the room, filled with anger and pain. Jack wanted to make it clear that he had no sympathy for the men who had caused so much suffering to his family. The atmosphere in the room turned tense as Jack's words lingered, cutting through the prisoners' defenses.

Jack takes his fist and punches both K-9 and Da-Bo in the head a couple of times each.

Jack turned to one of the guards and commanded, "Tell the doctor to give them painkillers so they don't die from shock."

The guard nodded and quickly left the room to relay Jack's orders to the prison doctor. Despite his rage and thirst for revenge, Jack knew he had to ensure that the prisoners received medical attention to prevent any fatal consequences from their injuries. He wanted them to suffer, but not to the point of death– at least not yet.

Jack continued, addressing the other prisoners as he walked away, "They are yours now, do what you want with them. But don't kill them because if any of you do, then I'll kill you!" He made it clear that he wanted the prisoners to exact their revenge, but not to the point of ending their lives.

Turning his attention to Jerry, he added, "After the guys are finished with them, have them patched up and brought to my office. I'm going to keep them there for a while. I heard there is a hit out on them, and I don't want anybody to kill them. I don't want them getting off that easy. They're going to suffer for what they did to my wife and family."

With a cold determination, Jack walked away, leaving the prisoners to carry out their own brand of justice on K-9 and Da-Bo. He knew that his plan for revenge was far from over, and he intended to make them pay for their heinous crimes in the most painful way possible.

XVIII

As Jack walks out the door, several guards follow him closely, creating a sense of anticipation among the prisoners. The atmosphere is charged as the inmates surround K-9 and Da-Bo, their attention focused on the unfolding situation. The door closes, leaving the audience wondering what will transpire in this crucial moment.

Inside the lunchroom at 11:45 AM, the space is bustling with prisoners enjoying their meals. Among them is the prisoner who found Razor's ring; he now proudly wears it on his finger, seemingly oblivious to its significance. As he walks past some of Razor's gang members, including Dyno, one of them catches sight of the familiar ring. A spark of recognition glimmers in his eyes, hinting at the potential implications of this discovery.

Just as the tension grows within the lunchroom, Jack and his guards make their entrance, drawing the attention of all the inmates. The room falls silent, with all eyes fixed on the warden and the unfolding events.

There is a moment of suspense and uncertainty, as Jack's presence in the lunchroom suggests that significant developments are about to unfold. The audience is left on the edge of their seats, eager to see how this confrontation will play out and how the discovery of the ring may impact the dynamics within the prison.

Razor's gang member 1 said, "That's Razor's ring he's wearing, and I want to know where he got it from."

Dyno mumbled to himself after seeing the ring, "Oh shit!"

Jack is close enough to hear the conversation and calls for backup guards to meet in the lunchroom.

Razor's gang member 1 approached the prisoner wearing the ring and demanded, "Hey, you! Where in the hell did you get that ring?"

The prisoner retorted, "None of your damn business."

Dyno, another member of Razor's gang, intervened, asking, "What's going on here?"

RAZOR'S GANG MEMBER 2 threatened the prisoner, "That's right, man! Because if you don't tell us, we're gonna kick your ass!"

The prisoner replied, "Alright then, if you have to know. I was eating some meatloaf, and I found the ring inside."

DYNO responded, "That's bullshit! You probably killed him by losing him in the grinder. That's why no one has heard or seen him since. Think about it. When was the last time anyone here found anything of value in the food that they were eating? Huh? Nobody, right? Right! You killed Razor and stole his ring!"

The prisoner insisted, "Look! I didn't kill anybody. I'm telling the truth!"

RAZOR'S GANG MEMBER 2 suggested, "Should we kill him right now?"

DYNO intervened, "No! Now is not the time. There are too many people around, and the warden is only a few feet away. And you know he's not joking about putting anyone in that microwave. Just lay low, and we'll get him."

Jack showed a sign of relief. Just then, guards came rushing into the lunchroom. There were more guards than the prisoners had ever seen, and David was with them.

David reported, "As you can see, Sir, all of the new guards from the other prisons are here and ready for duty."

Jack smiled and replied, "Yes, I see!"

Amidst the bustling activity in the prison, a prisoner mutters in frustration, "Damn! If we were thinking about a riot, we couldn't do it now with all of these armed guards."

Inside the medical ward, Jerry and his guards enter with K-9 and Da-Bo. Otis Bush, the medical attendant, notices the beaten prisoners and wears a disgusted expression.

"Don't tell me that Jack did this?" Otis asks with concern.

"Well! I won't tell you," Jerry responds evasively.

Otis looks around the medical ward, observing the numerous prisoners with casts and crutches due to Jack's violent actions. "This has got to stop. Hell, I'm running out of bandages. Take a look around. Look at all of the prisoners he's beaten the hell out of!" he exclaims, frustrated by the ongoing brutality.

"I need to have a talk with him right now. Is he in his office?" Otis inquires, eager to confront Jack about the escalating situation.

"I think so," Jerry replies, uncertain about the warden's current whereabouts.

Otis instructs a nurse to tend to K-9 and Da-Bo while he goes to find Jack and address the issue. He walks out with determination, seeking a solution to the growing turmoil in the prison.

Meanwhile, inside Jack's office, the warden is engaged in a conversation with Carl.

"I was able to get in contact with Mr. Yosoto, and he will be here sometime tomorrow to discuss his employment with us," Carl informs Jack about the upcoming meeting.

"Great. How much money do we have in our accounts?" Jack asks, focused on the financial matters.

"In our personal accounts, we have 20 million each, and in the state's account, there is half a billion dollars!" Carl replies, highlighting their significant funds.

"Good! That'll be more than enough to finish out the year, to pay everyone's salary, fix the highways, and whatever else needs to be done," Jack declares, relieved about their financial stability.

Just then, Otis Bush enters Jack's office, his face expressing his disapproval and concern about the escalating violence and injuries among the prisoners. The situation in the prison has become increasingly tense, and Otis is determined to address it with the warden.

"Jack, I remember what you said before, but this beating the hell out of the prisoners has got to stop. And furthermore…" Otis said, his voice filled with concern and frustration.

"You are right," Jack replied unexpectedly, causing Otis to look surprised at his response.

(Surprised) "What? Did I hear you right?" Otis asked, trying to process Jack's sudden change of heart.

"You sure did. You see, they're going to be a lot more valuable to me being healthy," Jack explained, his tone calmer now, as if he had come to a decision.

"What do you mean by that?" Otis inquired, intrigued yet cautious.

"I'm having a Japanese surgeon come in tomorrow who can attach human body parts to a person that has lost theirs. You're going to help him with whatever he needs, and there will be lots of money in it for you," Jack revealed, a glint of ambition in his eyes.

Otis shook his head, unable to believe what he was hearing. "Jack! I can't be a part of this. Come on, Son, don't you think you've done enough?"

Jack abruptly stood up, his anger flaring. "Don't you tell me what you won't do. You're going to be a part of this whether you like it or not!"

"And if I don't?" Otis questioned, standing his ground despite the intimidation.

"Well, Otis, I don't know what happened to $100,000 of the state's money, and we checked everyone's account that works here. We found out that you are $100,000 richer! Now, how did that happen?" Jack accused, his voice rising in accusation."I'll tell you how it happened. You transferred the money to your account. Now, if you play ball with me, you can keep the money. But if you don't, Carl will prosecute your ass, and you'll find yourself laying on the operating table instead of operating on it. Do you understand?"

Otis remained silent, his face conflicted with fear and uncertainty.

"Do you understand?" Jack demanded, asserting his dominance.

Otis finally nodded his head, not daring to speak.

"Now get your ass out of here," Jack ordered, dismissing him harshly.

As Otis turned to leave, Jack called him back, showing no remorse.

"Oh, by the way, don't ever call me Son again. Now leave," Jack added, the finality in his voice leaving no room for further discussion.

Otis left the office, feeling trapped and cornered by Jack's power and influence.

"Why don't you just let him quit?" Carl questioned, concerned for his friend.

"I don't want him to get out of here and start running his mouth. It may bring added attention, and we don't need that," Jack explained, his mind always calculating the potential consequences of his actions.

XIX

The next day, inside the prison, a sense of anticipation fills the air as the prisoners whom Jack had promised to set free are gathered in his office. Dressed in street clothes, their eyes are filled with a mix of hope and apprehension.

Jack, seated behind his desk, takes a moment to observe the group before him. His expression reflects a mix of determination and fulfillment, knowing that he is about to fulfill his commitment to these men.

"Here is the money that I promised you guys," Jack announced, handing each of them a check for $50,000. "Thanks for the good job, fellas, and I hope that I don't see any one of you back in here."

Mutt Dog, looking at his check, expressed his gratitude, "I can't believe that you kept your word. Thank you very much."

The other prisoners also thanked Jack before

leaving the office. However, as they were leaving, Jack called Dyno back.

"What is it, Warden?" Dyno asked, curious about the sudden summoning.

Jack pulled out another check from his drawer, this time for $10,000, and handed it to Dyno.

"This is for what you did in the lunchroom the other day," Jack explained. "That could have been a total screw-up, maybe even a riot afterward."

Dyno looked surprised and thankful, "Thank you. I get a second chance at life, plus $60,000. I'm making sure nothing happens!"

"Okay, be good and get your ass out of here," Jack says to Dyno.

Dyno nods appreciatively, acknowledging Jack's words, and leaves the office. With Dyno gone, Jerry wheels in K-9, and another guard brings in Da-Bo, both prisoners looking battered and bandaged from the previous altercation.

"Where do you want them?" Jerry asks.

"Put them on the right side of my desk," Jack instructs.

Jerry carefully positions K-9 and Da-Bo as directed, then leaves the office, leaving Jack alone with the two injured prisoners. Jack takes a moment to look at some papers on his desk before deciding to walk over to the file cabinet. While filing the papers, he glances at K-9 and Da-Bo, who are slumped over and mumbling in pain.

Suddenly, Jack slaps both K-9 and Da-Bo three times each to get their attention. The impact causes them to stir and groan, their injuries evident from their pained reactions. Jack eyes them with a hint of sadistic satisfaction, knowing that they are now at his mercy.

The room falls silent as Jack contemplates his next move. The tense atmosphere lingers, and Jack's expression reveals his determination to make them suffer for the pain they caused him and his family.

"What! What! You two punks better get used to it. Because if I don't personally punch you two motherfuckers at least fifty times a day, consider it a miracle. Oh, by the way, I have some good news. I have ordered you all some pantyhose to match your dresses. HA! HA!" Jack's sadistic laughter echoed through the room, sending shivers down the spines of Da-Bo and K-9.

Tears streamed down Da-Bo and K-9's faces, their spirits crushed under the weight of Jack's relentless torment. Despite their pain and fear, Jack showed no mercy, relishing in their suffering. His sinister glee only fueled his desire to inflict more pain upon them.

With a malicious grin, Jack continued, "Want something to cry about? I'll give you something to cry about. You two remember those nice guys I left you with the other day, don't you?" His chilling words hung in the air as K-9 and Da-Bo looked up at Jack, filled with dread at the thought of what was to come.

"Well, they've been asking about you all, so guess what? You're going to see them again, but not just today, every day! So you all might as well get used to it, just in case you all forgot. HA! HA!" Jack's sadistic laughter echoed in the room as he relished the fear he instilled in K-9 and Da-Bo. The two prisoners trembled in terror, fully aware of the torment that awaited them at the hands of the cruel warden.

Jack continued his sinister tirade, enjoying the power he had over the helpless prisoners. Da-Bo and K-9 had tears streaming down their faces as Jack's words sank in. With each slap, their pain intensified, and they could only whimper in agony.

Amidst the torment, Jack's phone rang. He picked it up, still smirking, and answered, "Hello Jerry!"

Jerry's voice came through the receiver, "I'm here, sir."

"K-9 and Da-Bo are ready to go see their boyfriends," Jack said, his voice dripping with malice.

"I'll be right there, sir," Jerry replied, understanding the cruel fate that awaited the two prisoners.

Jerry soon arrived with guards, escorting the injured K-9 and Da-Bo out of the office. As they left, Mr. Yosoto, the Japanese surgeon, took a seat before Jack. The man had an air of authority and respect about him.

"It's a pleasure to meet you, Mr. Yosoto," Jack said, extending his hand.

Mr. Yosoto stood up and bowed respectfully. "Likewise, Mr. Blake."

Cutting straight to the point, Jack asked, "Let's get right to it. How much money do you want?"

But Mr. Yosoto had a different agenda in mind. "It's not a question of money, Mr. Blake. I'm already a rich man. I just want to perform what I think can be a great help to mankind. Just give me 10% of whatever you make off of this deal."

Intrigued, Jack considered the offer for a moment before accepting with a handshake. Little did he know that this collaboration would lead to unimaginable consequences within the prison walls.

SIX MONTHS LATER: INSIDE THE PRISON- LUNCHROOM:

The lunchroom was a stark reminder of the brutal transformation that had taken place under Jack's rule. Many prisoners were now missing limbs, and the once defiant atmosphere had turned into one of fear and submission.

As a prisoner stood on a table and called for rebellion, the others hesitated, unsure if they could withstand Jack's wrath. The fear in their eyes was palpable.

But another prisoner rose to speak, warning them of Jack's new sinister agenda. The words struck a chord with everyone present, and they scrambled to flee the lunchroom in a desperate attempt to avoid becoming Jack's next victims.

Jack had achieved complete control over the prisoners, instilling fear and compliance, making it clear that resistance was futile. In his reign of terror, the once rebellious inmates had become his pawns, trapped in a cruel game orchestrated by the sadistic warden.

The Keeper of the Castle

※

Amidst the chaos and tension, the prisoner on the table yelled urgently, "Hey everybody, the warden is coming. Run!"

The warning echoed through the lunchroom, and prisoners scrambled in all directions, bumping into each other and knocking over chairs and tables. Fear spread like wildfire, and the atmosphere became charged with panic.

In the midst of the mayhem, another prisoner stood up and took charge, his voice determined and defiant. "Fuck this shit! We got to make a stand right now! I don't care how many guards he has!" he exclaimed, rallying his fellow inmates.

The lunchroom erupted with unified chants of "YA! YA!" as prisoners agreed with the call to take a stand against the oppressive warden. Even those who were physically limited joined in, expressing their resolve to fight back.

The prisoner in the wheelchair, missing limbs but not his spirit, added with determination, "That's right! He can't take anything else from me but my left arm. To hell with him."

However, another voice rose above the clamor, bringing the prisoners to a somber realization. The prisoner on the table, attempting to quell the growing rebellion, made a startling revelation, "Wait a minute! You don't understand, he's not looking for an arm or a leg this time. He's looking for somebody's penis! I don't know about any of you, he's not going to get mine, and if you hang around here long enough, he may just get yours. You all have been warned!"

The lunchroom fell into an eerie silence, prisoners looking at each other in shock and fear. The once defiant atmosphere now gave way to apprehension and uncertainty. The reality of the warden's sadistic actions left them paralyzed with fear.

Suddenly, prisoners started running in every direction, trying to escape the impending doom. Crutches were abandoned, and some prisoners stumbled and fell, desperate to put as much distance as possible between themselves and the menacing warden.

Outside the lunchroom, chaos ensued, and Jack, accompanied by his guards and the patient, observed the frantic scene. He couldn't comprehend why the prisoners had disappeared so quickly.

PRISONER IN WHEELCHAIR

"Well, at least I still have that. Let me get the hell out of here," he said, wheeling his chair as fast as he could with his one arm.

All of the prisoners were running into each other, trying to escape. Some were falling down and losing their crutches.

INSIDE THE HALLWAY:

Jack walked down the hallway with his guards and the patient who was looking for the sex organ. The patient had a big smile on his face, while Jack had a crazy look on his face.

"Thank God! I thought my sex life was over!" the patient exclaimed.

"It just may be a new beginning. You just might get something attached to you that is larger than life!" Jack said with an evil grin.

"Well, all right!" the patient replied eagerly.

As Jack opened the lunchroom door, he saw a prisoner running out of another door. The lunchroom was empty. Jack had a strange look on his face.

"Isn't this the time the inmates eat lunch?" he asked.

"Yes, Sir," replied the guard.

"Where did they all go?" Jack wondered, moving his head strangely.

"Darn! Are you sure I'm going to be able to get one?" the patient asked nervously.

"I'm positive. I know the perfect one for you," Jack assured him.

Inside jack's office, Da-Bo and K-9 are sitting in Jack's office in wheelchairs. They're both missing their hands and their feet. K-9 is missing one of his eyes. They're all beat up from Jack punching on them all the time. Da-Bo has a sign on him that says, "I am a fag" and K-9, sitting right next to Da-Bo, has a sign on that says "me too". Jack walks in with his guards and the patient.

"Jerry! Please take Da-Bo to the roof. His boyfriends are waiting." Jack said, turning to Jerry.

Jerry wheels Da-Bo out of the office.

Jack turned to K-9)

I have some good news and some bad news. The good news is that you're going with Da-Bo to get it up the ass today, but the bad news is that this man is going to get your penis! HA! HA!

K-9's face turned pale with horror, and he stammered in fear, "NO! NO! NO!"

"Shut up! Just shut up!" Jack screamed and punched K-9 eight times in the face.

K-9 drops his head. The patient is looking at this in shock.

"Maybe this isn't a good idea?" The patient said as he looked at K9's condition.

"Look here! Do you want this operation or not? This is the fool that raped my wife! And killed my family. That's why I treat him the way that I do. And I know for a fact that he is B positive, just like you so tell me what is going on with you?" Jack replied furiously.

"I'm sorry Governor, I didn't know this was they guy? I'll gladly take his penis from him since he doesn't know the proper, respectful way to use it." The patient responded.

"Well okay, it's as good as yours!" Jack said and gave a sinister laugh.

He then turned to the guard and said, "Take this man and K-9 to the medical ward where the surgery can be performed."

"Yes Sir." The guard replied respectfully.

As the guard is wheeling K-9 out, Jack turns around and punches him in the back of the head three times. Carl walked in as soon as the guard left.

"Good! Just the man I wanted to see. So tell me Carl, how much money do we have in our personal accounts?" Jack asked, expecting to have millions in one go.

"We have $20 million," Carl replied calmly.

But Jack's reaction was far from expected. "Is that all? Damn!" he exclaimed, frustration evident in his voice.

Carl looks at Jack like he's crazy, for a minute, then starts talking.

Jack's anger was palpable, and he clenched his fists tightly. He glared at Carl, his eyes burning with frustration and impatience. "Well, spit it out then! What is it that I won't like?" he demanded, his voice trembling with anger.

Carl took a deep breath, steeling himself to deliver the unsettling news. "The prisoners that we have left, their blood types are not matching up with the people that we have waiting to receive their body parts," he revealed, his tone serious and grave.

At Carl's words, Jack's face turned even redder with rage. He felt like the ground beneath him was crumbling, realizing the implications of the situation. This wasn't just a minor setback; it was a colossal problem that threatened everything they had worked for.

He couldn't contain his frustration any longer. Jack jumped up from his seat and grabbed his stick, pounding it against the file cabinet in a fit of anger, releasing a string of curses. "Fuck, shit, fuck, shit, fuck, shit!" he yelled, the sound echoing through the room.

Carl took a few steps backward, startled by Jack's outburst. He had never seen him like this before. Jack was usually the composed and level-headed one, but now he seemed like a man possessed.

Carl watched Jack with growing concern as he wreaked havoc on the file cabinet. "Jack! Jack are you okay? What's wrong? We have $20 million a piece," Carl tried to reason with him.

Suddenly, Jack stopped, his gaze fixed on Carl. He crossed the room in a few strides, his expression wild. His outburst was startling, but more so was the sudden silence that followed.

"That's not enough. I want more. What happened? How come we don't have enough prisoners?" Jack questioned, his eyes boring into Carl's.

"Well, the microwave deal stopped a hell of a lot of crime. But when the word got out that you would stand a good chance of losing your body parts if you came to prison, well, the only thing people are doing now is getting traffic tickets and J-walking," Carl explained, a hint of laughter creeping into his voice.

Jack paused, processing what Carl said. A slow, almost manic smile spread across his face, and he again invaded Carl's personal space.

"That's it!" Jack exclaimed, his eyes lighting up with an idea.

Carl looked at Jack, taken aback. "What's it?"

"We'll go to the senate and have them pass a bill that anyone caught getting a traffic ticket or j-walking, gets 25 years in prison," Jack proposed, grinning widely. "What do you think?"

Carl was silent, staring at Jack as if he'd lost his mind. But Jack was persistent. "Well! What do you think?"

Jack's audacity finally pulled words from Carl. "Jack! You can't go around putting people in jail because of a traffic ticket or j-walking. I don't know why we're having this conversation; I know you're not serious."

As Carl voiced his disbelief, Jack stood there, his smile not fading. It was clear that the situation was far from being resolved. The tension lingered in the room, the silence punctuated only by the quiet rustle of papers in the battered file cabinet.

Carl, taken aback by Jack's sudden eruption, stared at him. There was a look of disbelief and concern etched on his face. He had known Jack for years, yet this unpredictable, volatile version of his friend felt foreign to him.

Glancing at his watch, Carl tried to break the palpable tension in the room. "Jack, can I get back to you on this? I'm running behind on my work, and it's getting late," he said, attempting to inject some normalcy into the conversation.

Jack, however, was far from calming down. "What the hell do you mean it's getting late? It's only 12:30 in the afternoon," he retorted, his words coming out as a growl. "I tell you what, I'll get that law passed by myself. You're turning on me, Carl; now get the hell out of my office before I beat the hell out of you with this stick!"

A wave of fear washed over Carl at Jack's threatening words, but he managed to keep his expression steady. The room fell into silence as Carl gave Jack an uncertain look, then exited, leaving Jack alone with his fury.

As he stepped out into the hallway, Carl spotted Jerry and David. With a nod, he made his way over to them. The two men greeted him, their friendly tones in stark contrast to the hostility he'd just left behind.

"How are you guys doing today?" Carl asked, trying to push the recent interaction with Jack to the back of his mind.

"Fine, and yourself?" Jerry and David responded in unison.

"Fine, fine," Carl replied. "But what I want to talk to you all about is Jack. Has he been acting a little strange to you too?"

"We were just talking about that before you came up," David admitted, concern etched onto his features.

Jerry chimed in, "I don't know what has gotten into him. He's like a madman sometimes."

David nodded in agreement. "He sure is. I remember when we used to talk, now he's just bossy and rude and mean. He even threatened to hit me with the stick last month."

Their shared concern was clear. Jack's behavior was spiraling, and it was leaving a trail of unease in its wake. They knew they had to do something, yet the question remained- what was triggering these outbursts, and how could they help their friend before things went too far? The weight of the situation bore heavily on them as they stood in the quiet hallway, the uncertainty hanging in the air like a dark cloud.

Carl chuckled and shook his head as he shared his encounter with someone named Jack. "He just told me the same thing if I didn't get out of his office. Is Doctor Otis Bush here today?" he inquired.

Jerry confirmed, "Yes, he is. Why?"

Carl recalled a haunting memory, "I remembered when Jack's family was killed, and he said this was going to start happening. He called it some kind of a disease. Nobody ever heard of it, and we all thought that he was crazy. But now I'm not so sure. Maybe someone should have listened to him."

David reassured, "It is never too late. Let's go have a talk with him now."

"After you," Carl gestured.

Inside the Medical Ward, Otis, David, Jerry, and Carl engaged in a serious discussion.

"Are you telling me that Jack actually said he was going to hit you guys with his stick?" Otis asked, surprised.

"That's what we're saying," David confirmed.

"Well, you better be lucky that he didn't do it in his state of mind. The next time he probably will," Otis warned.

Concerned, Carl asked, "What can we do? Can we get him some help?"

"It's too late for that," Otis replied solemnly.

Refusing to accept defeat, Carl said, "Come on! There's something we can do. He's talking about giving anyone that gets a traffic ticket or caught j-walking 25 years in prison."

Jerry and David laughed, but Otis remained serious. "You can't be serious," Jerry remarked.

"Oh! He is very serious," Carl affirmed.

Otis issued a chilling warning, "And don't be surprised if he gets that into law."

Now, with worried expressions, Jerry, David, and Carl reconsidered their options.

"Otis, there has got to be something we can do," David pleaded.

"The only thing I can think of at this point is to kill him," Otis shockingly suggested.

Carl and Jerry were taken aback by Otis' proposal.

The Moral Dilemma

"We can't kill him! Are you crazy?" Carl objected.

"I agree. We can't do that," David added.

"Mark my words, if I don't, you are going to wish that you did," Otis stated ominously. Jerry sought clarity, "What do you mean by that? And what is this disease that you said that Jack is suffering from?"

Otis revealed, "Jack is suffering from post-traumatic stress syndrome. It's a war disease like being shell-shocked. It usually happens when tragedy occurs in your life that you can't get over. A lot of prisoners are suffering from this too because of the hard life they had growing up."

Jerry pressed further, "Tell me why we have to kill Jack? You don't have to kill anyone else that has this disease."

"Jack needs to see a shrink. That's the first step to recovery, but we all know he's not going to do that. Jack is getting worse by the minute. He has become too powerful, and that's what I was afraid of. Now, we got a mad man in total control, and that's the only way to bring him down," explained Otis.

"Are you sure about this?" Carl questioned hesitantly.

"You're damn right I'm sure. Carl, you're almost as much to blame for the way Jack is as Jack himself. Being chief prosecuting attorney, you could've stopped him from passing some of the laws, instead of helping him. Because of this, Jack now has power and money, and that's hard to fight, fellas," accused Otis.

As the gravity of their situation settled in, the group found themselves grappling with the enormity of their responsibility and the difficult path they must now navigate.

❦

"Can't we find a way to make him step down or force him to resign?" Davis said.

"Hell no! Jack has too many friends and he is too powerful. The people in Missouri are behind him 100%. I mean, look at the big picture, Jack is credited for bringing Missouri's crime rate down to less than 1% and giving the people of Missouri a couple of kickbacks, which nobody has ever done before, not to mention paying off the senate to get his laws passed. Everyone loves this guy and he slowly is becoming a nationwide personality. The prisoners and us four are the only ones who know how crazy Jack really is. It took you guys nearly two years to understand what I'm talking about and you guys work closely with him. Now, try telling someone that Jack has a problem that doesn't know him that well, or someone that's only see him on TV. They're going to tell you all that you're crazy like they told me!" Otis said, he was well aware of the power Jack's power.

"You're right about a lot of things, Otis, but I don't think killing Jack is the answer." Jerry Replied.

"I agree with Jerry." David said agreeing to Jerry's point.

"So do I." Carl nodded his head.

"Well, whatever you all come up with, please don't let him find out that you're plotting to get him out of office because if he finds out, not only will you guys be out of a job, but you just might end up on this operating table."

Otis warned them. He didn't want them to get in any kind of trouble.

※

ANGLE ON OPERATING TABLE- Carl, David and Jerry are looking at it.

The next day, on Friday twelve noon Carl is walking by and Senator John is walking outside the senate. Beck calls him. Carl stops to see what he wants.

"Hey there Carl! How's it going?" John greeted him, keeping a smile in his face.

"Fine and yourself." Carl replied.

"Good! Good! How come you're not with the Governor today?" Beck asked curiously.

"What do you mean?" Carl asked. He was quite confused about why Beck asked him such questions.

"He called us all together so he could pass a bill into law, that all traffic offenders and j-walkers would get 25 years in prison. HA! HA! Isn't that a laugh?" Beck replied trying to sound sarcastic.

"You all didn't pass it did you?" Carl asked, giving him a serious look.

"Sure we did. He even offered us one million dollars to split among ourselves if we passed the bill. But we didn't take the money because we all knew nobody is going to enforce it, and he had to be joking anyway. HA! HA! What a sense of humor." Beck said, he was quite nervous by now and couldn't understand how to react.

Carl puts his hands over his face and looks John Beck in the eye.

"He's not joking?" Carl told him and walked away fast. As for John Beck, he stood there stunned.

On the roof, Da-Bo is sitting in his wheelchair. He's crying and mumbling to himself.

"I can't take this anymore! I can't take this anymore!" Da-Bo said angrily.

On the roof, the other prisoners seem indifferent to the distressing scene involving Da-Bo. They sit at a table, engrossed in a card game, while the three-story high prison block looms in the background.

Inside Jack's office, located within the confines of the prison, a gentle knocking sound resonates through the dimly lit room, prompting Jack to look up from his desk.

"Come in," he calls out in response to the visitor at the door.

The door opens, and it's Sally, Jerry's wife. She's wearing a nice tight-fitting dress. Jack's eyes show a hint of lust as he looks at her. He had lust in his eyes.

"Hello, Jack. How are you doing?" Sally smiled warmly and greeted him as she stepped further into the office.

Caught off guard by her sudden appearance, Jack found himself momentarily speechless. Sally, with her radiant smile and the elegant dress that perfectly complemented her graceful figure, had an aura about her that could lighten even the tensest atmospheres.

"Fine, and yourself?" Jack finally managed to reply, trying his best to maintain a casual demeanor.

"I'm doing very well, thank you," Sally responded. She seemed oblivious to the tension Jack was still trying to shake off. "I came here to drop off the keys to Jerry. Would you make sure he gets them?"

"Sure, I will," Jack nodded. However, before she could turn to leave, he found himself voicing a concern he'd been harboring for a while. "But before you leave, I need to talk to you about Jerry."

Sally paused, her smile fading slightly as she turned back to face him. "What's the problem?"

The room seemed to grow quieter as Jack met her gaze. He knew the conversation they were about to have wouldn't be an easy one.

"Are you all having money problems?" Jack asked cautiously. His tone was gentle, not wanting to alarm her but at the same time needing to address what he'd noticed.

The question hung in the air between them, a tangible pause following his words. Sally's smile had faded completely now, replaced by a look of surprise. Yet, her eyes held no hint of fear or worry, only the calm resilience that Jack had always admired in her. It was clear that she would answer his question, but Jack could only wonder what the response would be.

"Yes, but it's nothing that we can't work out." Sally replied.

"Well, I hate to tell you this, but Jerry has been stealing from our accounts and we may have to prosecute him. If so, we would have to sell his body parts to make up for what he's stolen. But I'm willing to make a deal with you." Jack told Sally, his intentions were not what they might seem.

"What deal?" Sally asked giving him a strange look. She was quite uncomfortable.

Jack reaches into one of his drawers and pulls out an envelope full of cash. Jack gets up out of his seat and walks over to where Sally is.

"It's $10,000 in here and you can have it. I will drop the charges on Jerry if you will make love to me." Jack said. He didn't even stammer while saying such thing.

Jack gets behind Sally and starts rubbing his hands up and down her arms and kissing her on the neck. Sally is scared and shaking a little.

"What if I don't agree to do this?" Sally asked him. She wasn't sure what was just happening with her.

"I already told you. I will have him dissected like a frog and take his reproductive organs so he won't be any good to you anyway." Jack threatened her.

Sally starts to cry as Jack is undressing her.

"You promise not to do anything to him?" Sally asked him worriedly.

"I promise." Jack said, he was still too much focused on undressing her.

On the roof, Da-Bo rocks himself out of his wheelchair and rolls himself off the roof, killing himself when he hits the ground. The other prisoners get up from playing cards when they hear Da-Bo hit the ground.

"The warden is going to be pissed off. Why wasn't somebody watching him?" Prisoner 1 voiced the question that was on everyone's mind. The prison was supposed to be a place of strict surveillance and security, yet somehow, Da-Bo managed to find an opportunity to kill himself

Inside Jack's office, Sally is putting on her clothes and Jack is getting dressed too. Sally is crying and holding the envelope with the money in her hand. The phone rings and Jack answers.

"Hello!" Jack said, immediately after receiving the call.

"This is Jerry, sir. I'm calling to tell you that Francis Johnson just rolled off the roof and killed himself, and K-9 died on the operating table today." Jerry answered, unaware of the fact that Jack forced his wife to make love with him.

"Well, maybe they are in HELL right now." Jack chuckled and said.

"Are you coming down, sir?" Jerry asked.

※

No, I'm not. I'm a little busy right now. Please handle the situation for me." Jack said, looking at Jerry's wife.

Jack's words were firm, his attention focused on the myriad tasks that demanded his immediate attention. Jerry's wife, well acquainted with the gravity of Jack's role as the warden, understood that he often had to contend with critical matters within the prison.

She nodded understandingly, offering a reassuring smile. "Of course, Jack. I understand. I'll take care of it."

Jack hung up the phone and Sally starts to walk out of the office when Jack stops her.

"Wait one minute Sally." He said.

Sally stops and Jack walks over to her and snatches the money out of her hand.

"I'm sorry but I'm going to take this back. You just weren't that good." Jack said and passed on a sick smile to her.

"You son of a bitch!" Sally said out loud, she was outrageous for what happened. That made Jack so angry that he hit Sally in the face with his fist.

"Now get your ass out of here you slut, bitch!" Jack shouted angrily.

Sally turned and ran out of the door crying.

An hour later, Jack is sitting down talking to a man seated next to him when there's a knock at the door.

"Come on in." Jack said.

Carl enters the office, a serious expression on his face.

"Jack, we need to talk." Carl said. He sounded quite serious at that time.

"Yes, we sure do but first I want you to meet someone that just came on staff. Victor Grant meet Carl Davis." Jack replied.

Victor and Carl shook hands.

Jack was quick to interject, eager to clarify the situation, "Oh, I can answer that, Carl. He's your replacement!"

Carl was taken aback by the abruptness of Jack's announcement, "WHAT!" he exclaimed, his surprise palpable in the silent room.

Victor, sensing the tension and recognizing the need for a private discussion between Jack and Carl, silently exited the room after Jack requested, "You heard me; please excuse us for a minute, Victor."

"What in the hell do you mean he's my replacement?" Carl asked in disbelief.

"You are fired, Carl! You wouldn't back me on the bill I wanted passed. You turned on me, Carl, and I don't need anyone like you. Here is your pay, lying on the desk. Take it and leave." Jack said and he sounded quite seriously.

Carl grabs the envelope and opens it and sees a check for $1,500. Carl is pissed off. With the door closing behind Victor, Carl turned his attention back to Jack. His face was a picture of disbelief as he processed the shocking news, while Jack sat across from him, maintaining a steady gaze, ready to handle the difficult conversation that lay ahead.

"Where is the rest of my money?" Carl asked him. He was quite shocked to see it.

"If you are talking about the $20 million, I decided to keep it. Now get out of here!" Jack said aggressively.

"You can't do that. My name is on the account too." Carl said aggressively.

"I'm glad you brought that up because I'm going to the bank tomorrow and have that changed. Damn! I can't do it tomorrow, it's Labor Day and the banks are closed. I'll do it the first thing Monday morning." Jack responded.

A look of shock crossed Carl's face as he processed Jack's words. "You can't do this?" He asked, his voice reflecting his disbelief.

"Oh yes, I can. Remember, I'm the Governor. Who's going to stop me?" Jack retorted, a smug grin appearing on his face.

Carl's eyes narrowed, anger evident in his voice, "I think I'm going to kick your ass right now."

At Carl's threatening words, Jack acted swiftly, "Guards!" he yelled.

At his command, eight guards promptly rushed into Jack's office. Jack gave Carl a pointed look, a satisfied chuckle escaping him, "I thought you would react this way. So when you showed up, I had the guards waiting by the door." He addressed the guards, "Please show Mr. Davis to the door."

The guards escorted Carl out of the office, and Victor, who had been waiting outside, stepped back in.

Jack, now addressing Carl as he was being taken away, announced, "Come back Sunday night and clean out your office. Now take him away."

As the door closed behind Carl, the tension in the room lifted slightly, but the echo of their heated argument still lingered. The events that unfolded had set a new tone in their relationship, marking a significant shift in their power dynamics.

SATURDAY MORNING- LABOR DAY- INSIDE JERRY'S HOUSE:

The warm aroma of breakfast filled the air as Sally stood in the kitchen, busy preparing a delicious morning meal. The clatter of pans and the sizzle of bacon filled the cozy space, setting the scene for a delightful Labor Day breakfast.

Jerry, just waking up, walked into the kitchen with a smile on his face. Sneaking up behind Sally, he wrapped his arms around her, giving her a gentle hug. Sally jumped.

"Good morning," Jerry whispered into her ear, his voice filled with love.

꽃

Sally didn't respond, her focus resolutely on the breakfast she was preparing. There was a determined set to her shoulders, and she avoided Jerry's gaze, increasing his sense of unease.

"Turn around, baby, and give me a kiss." Jerry implored, hoping to break the tension.

Despite his request, Sally didn't turn around. Jerry could sense her hesitation and it was starting to agitate him.

"What in the hell is wrong with you?" Jerry burst out, unable to contain his frustration any longer.

In a swift motion, Jerry turned her around and his confusion turned into shock. There, marring her face, was a black eye. The sight was jarring, filling Jerry with a sense of dread and anger.

"Who did this to you?" Jerry demanded, anger flashing in his eyes.

Sally remained silent, tears welling up in her eyes. She tried to hold them back but couldn't, and they spilled down her cheeks. Seeing her distress, Jerry pulled her into a comforting embrace, his anger momentarily forgotten.

After a few moments, he gently released her, holding her at arm's length. He looked her directly in the eye, his expression serious. "Now, tell me who did this and why?" Jerry asked, his voice firm but caring.

Sally hesitated, her eyes downcast. After a few seconds of silence, she finally spoke up. "Okay… your boss; the Warden or Governor did this." Her voice was barely a whisper, but it echoed loudly in the silent kitchen.

"Why?" Jerry asked her. He was frustrated with what she just said, but he wanted to know the reason.

"He raped me, in a way!" Sally finally told her husband, the harassment she faced.

※

Jerry's anger surged as he processed Sally's revelation. His face contorted with rage, and he struggled to contain the torrent of emotions welling up inside him.

"What do you mean by that?" Jerry repeated, his voice trembling with a mix of anger and disbelief. He couldn't fathom how someone in a position of power, especially his boss, could commit such a heinous act.

"He told me that you had been stealing and if I didn't have sex with him he was going to prosecute you and have you dissected like a frog. Please forgive me Jerry, I didn't want to do it but I was so scared that he was going to hurt you and that I would never see you again. Please forgive me?" Sally said and also asked for forgiveness.

Jerry held Sally close, his upset evident as he tried to comfort her. "I understand, it's not your fault," he murmured, his voice filled with empathy and love.

As the reality of the situation sank in, Jerry's emotions swirled into a raging storm. "I'm going to kill him myself. Otis was right; I should have listened to him!" he declared, his anger and regret blending into one powerful force.

Driven by a potent mix of fury and determination, Jerry quickly got dressed, his mind set on confronting the one responsible for harming his beloved wife. His thoughts were filled with the need for justice and retribution.

He rushed out of the house, his footsteps heavy with purpose. His heart pounded in his chest as he navigated the path ahead, his mind set on confronting the Warden or Governor for the unthinkable act committed against Sally.

In the heat of the moment, he was driven by raw emotion, but deep down, he knew that seeking revenge alone would not solve the problem. He needed a plan, support, and the strength to face such a powerful figure.

INSIDE THE PRISON- DAVID'S OFFICE:

David was engrossed in his work when Otis entered the room, his expression serious.

"What's going on, Otis?" David inquired, sensing that something was amiss.

Otis looked at him incredulously, "Don't you know?"

David shook his head, puzzled by Otis's question, "Know what?"

"That your son is locked up in here," Otis revealed, his tone laden with concern.

David's eyes widened in shock, "What!"

"Didn't anyone tell you?" Otis questioned, surprised by the lack of communication.

"Hell no! Where is he?" David asked urgently, already feeling a sense of dread.

"In the holdover, but you better do something to get him out fast. The paperwork has already been done, and he's scheduled to go on the operating table Monday morning," Otis warned, his worry evident.

David's frustration and anxiety mounted. "Are you kidding me? How in the hell did he get in here, and what did he do?" he demanded, his mind racing with questions and concern for his son.

"He ran a stop sign," Otis revealed, his voice steady despite the absurdity of the situation.

"What! Ran a stop sign and they locked him up for that?" David exclaimed, disbelief clear in his voice.

"Do you remember what Carl said about Jack wanting to pass that law for j-walkers and traffic offenders?" Otis asked, reminding David of an earlier conversation.

David nodded, the memory suddenly fresh in his mind. "Yeah! I remember."

"Not only did it pass, it is actually being enforced. Running a stop sign in Missouri carries a 25-year sentence and remember the law says that if you are in prison, you become property of the state. They can do anything they want with you, including taking your body parts," Otis explained grimly.

David paled at Otis's words. He couldn't believe what he was hearing.

Otis continued, "This is what is going to happen to your son if you don't do something about it now. I hate to say it, but if he does your son, you know you're going to be next, David. Jack knows you're not going to take that lying down and you all have the same blood type too."

David sat in shock, struggling to process everything Otis was telling him. "I just can't believe this. I got to do something," he murmured, his mind racing with thoughts of how he could protect his son.

"I told you what has to be done. There's no other way," Otis stated, his voice firm.

Just then, the door burst open and in stormed Jerry, clearly upset. David turned his attention to Jerry, alarmed by his state. "What is wrong with you?" David asked.

Jerry began pacing back and forth, his anger palpable. "Where in the hell is the warden? I went to his office but he's not there, and when I find him, I'm going to kill him!" Jerry blurted out.

David looked at Jerry, taken aback. "What did he do?"

"He told my wife a pack of lies that I was stealing and he was going to prosecute me if she did not have sex with him. So I guess you can call that rape and then he gave her a black eye!" Jerry roared, his rage barely contained. "I don't care what happens. As soon as I see him, I'm going to kill him!"

Otis chimed in, a knowing look on his face. "I hate to be the one who said I told you so, but you all wouldn't listen. Now maybe you all will listen this time."

"Okay, tell us what's on your mind," David requested, eager to hear Otis's plan.

"First thing is, Jerry, you have to calm down. Going out all gung-ho isn't the way to do it. We're going to lose him in the system like he has lost other people in the past," Otis advised. Turning to David, he asked, "Have you made out the schedule for the guards yet?"

David nodded, "I was going to do that now."

"Good! Have only a few guards scheduled for Sunday night. Let them work a few hours, then send them home.

That's going to be the night we set him up," Otis revealed his plan.

Jerry, who had been silent, finally spoke, "Don't you think that Jack will get a little suspicious if he doesn't see any guards?"

"No! Because here is the plan," Otis began, his voice filled with determination.

XX

Sunday night inside the Governor's Mansion, Jack's bedroom exudes an air of tranquility. The room is dimly lit, casting a warm glow across the elegant furnishings.

Jack was in bed, half drunk and fast asleep, sharing the bed with four naked women. The shrill ring of the phone cut through the silence, jolting him awake. Groggily, he picked up the phone and answered, "Hello!"

On the other end of the line, Otis's voice came through. "Sorry to have woken you, Jack, but you got to get here quick. The prisoners have gotten hold of some guns and say they'll kill the ten guards they're holding hostage. They want to talk to you right now!"

"Damn! Okay, I'll be right there. By the way, what are you doing there?" Jack questioned, struggling to shake off the alcohol-induced haze.

Otis hesitated for a moment before replying, "I came in to do some paperwork that I got behind on."

"Alright, tell them I'm on my way," Jack responded, attempting to pull himself together.

Otis added, "And by the way, there are no guards outside. They're all inside because of the uprising of the prisoners. Don't be surprised if you don't see any when you come in."

"Okay, thanks for telling me. Unlock the gate for me so that I can get in," Jack instructed, already getting dressed.

"Will do," Otis responded and hung up the phone.

Jack pulled up outside the prison, Otis waiting for him. As Jack got out of the car, Otis opened the gate.

"I'm glad you made it, Jack. They're getting restless," Otis greeted him, his voice laced with urgency.

"How did they get a hold of the guns?" Jack asked, his expression filled with confusion and disbelief.

"I don't know," Otis admitted, shaking his head.

The pair continued their walk towards the door. Upon reaching it, Otis held the door open for Jack, who walked in with Otis right behind him.

Once inside the prison, Jack's office was just a few feet from the door they had entered through.

"Where are they?" Jack asked, looking around the hallway.

"In your office," Otis responded, standing behind Jack.

"What!" Jack exclaimed in surprise.

Without another word, Otis quickly pushed Jack through the door into his office. David and Jerry were waiting for him inside.

"What in the hell is going on?" Jack demanded, scanning the room in confusion.

"This is what's going on," Jerry answered tersely, before punching Jack square in the face.

Jack fell to the floor, and Jerry loomed over him. "You bastard! You took advantage of my wife and beat her up!" Jerry accused, his voice raw with anger.

Jack managed to pick himself up off the floor but was quickly met with another punch, this time from David, causing him to fall back down.

"You were going to dissect my son. You know that if you were going to do him, you would have to do me too!" David spat out, his words seething with resentment.

ANGLE ON SPEAKERPHONE- Jack's eyes darted towards it as he struggled to get up from the floor.

"Wait a minute, you don't understand," Jack pleaded, trying to reason with Jerry and David.

In a desperate move, Jack made a fast break for the phone and managed to press the intercom button. "Guards! Guards!" he shouted urgently.

But Otis's revelation shattered any hope Jack had left. "It's no use, Jack; there are no guards here today," Otis calmly stated, pulling out a needle from his pocket. Fear began to grip Jack.

"What are you going to do with that?" Jack asked, his voice trembling with fear.

"You will see," Otis replied cryptically, turning to Jerry and David. "Hold him down."

David and Jerry wasted no time restraining Jack, overpowering his attempts to resist. Otis approached and without hesitation, injected the needle into Jack's arm. Jack struggled to stay on his feet, but soon, his strength waned, and he collapsed to the floor.

"Where are the bandages, so I can cover up his face?" Otis asked, breaking the tense silence.

David quickly handed over the requested items, and together, they worked to cover up Jack's identity.

"Let's hurry up and get him moved," Otis said, urgency in his voice. The three of them swiftly coordinated their efforts to transport Jack to a different location, away from his office.

Inside the medical ward, Jack is laying on the operating table, surrounded by four prisoners, each missing a limb. Two were without legs, and the other two were without arms. Jack wore nothing but his underwear, his face concealed under layers of bandages.

As Otis spoke to the prisoners, a sense of grim satisfaction passed between them. "At least you guys will be lucky enough to get back what was taken from you," Otis said, acknowledging their shared fate.

Mr. Yosoto, the surgeon, entered the room, and Otis greeted him warmly. "How are you doing, Mr. Yosoto? Warden Blake wanted me to tell you how much he appreciates you coming in this late at night to perform this operation."

"Oh, I will do anything for Governor Blake," Mr. Yosoto replied with a hint of reverence.

"Well! Let's get started," Otis declared, eager to proceed with their plan.

As Mr. Yosoto prepared to begin, he noticed the bandages covering Jack's face and inquired, "Why is the guy bandaged up?"

"A prisoner in the kitchen threw some boiling hot water in his face, and it burned him pretty bad," Otis quickly concocted a plausible explanation.

Mr. Yosoto nodded, seemingly satisfied with the answer. The room fell into a tense silence, each person aware of the dark secret that lay beneath the surface of this unusual operation.

INSIDE THE AUDITORIUM- FIVE O'CLOCK IN THE MORNING:

On stage, Otis, Jerry, David, and Jack all stood together. Jack was regaining consciousness, blinking awake in the harsh stage lights. He glanced around, taking in the crowd of prisoners seated before him. His gaze then landed on Otis, Jerry, and David.

"What in the hell is going on, and how come all of these prisoners are out here?" Jack asked, confusion clear on his face. He tried to move but quickly realized he couldn't. Looking down, Jack saw the horrific truth. He had no arms or legs. He let out a gasp, his eyes wide with shock.

"You can't do this to me! I'm the keeper of the castle, or did you all forget that I am also the Governor," Jack barked, trying to assert his authority despite the fear in his voice.

"In a few short minutes Jack, you were the Governor," Otis said with chilling calm.

"What do you mean by that?" Jack demanded, his voice shaking.

"Are you ready for the big show?" Otis asked, grabbing a microphone and addressing the crowd of prisoners.

The room erupted with cheers of agreement. Jerry pulled back the curtains, revealing a large object hidden behind them. The sight of it sent the prisoners into a wild frenzy, cheering and shouting with anticipation.

Jack's face drained of color. "No! No! Please do not do this!" he pleaded desperately, but his pleas fell on deaf ears.

"Sorry, Jack, but there is no other way," Otis said coldly.

What follows is a climactic moment in which Jack is subjected to a horrifying fate. The details of the event are too graphic and violent to describe, but suffice it to say the prisoners were jubilant. After the event concludes, Otis addresses the crowd again.

"No one is going to say a word about this, right?" he asked the prisoners.

"Right! Right! Right!" they chanted back, their voices echoing throughout the room.

Suddenly, Carl walked through the door. The prisoners fell silent, all eyes turning to him. The atmosphere was thick with tension and suspense as everyone awaited his reaction.

"What is going on in here, and where is Jack?" Carl asked, his eyes scanning the room as he stepped onto the stage.

Otis beckoned Carl to join him. As Carl approached, Otis went behind the microwave and pulled out what was left of Jack, presenting it to Carl.

"This is what is going on, and here is Jack," Otis announced grimly.

"I see that you all went ahead and killed him anyway," Carl stated, staring at the remains with a mixture of shock and revulsion.

"Yes, and the sad thing is that now we're going to have to do you the same way because you're the prosecuting attorney," Otis replied, his voice cold and emotionless.

Jerry and David moved swiftly, grabbing Carl. Carl struggled, but it was to no avail; he was firmly held in their grip.

"Wait a minute! Just wait a minute!" Carl protested, his face contorting with fear and anger. "Jack fired me the other day, and I'm no longer the prosecuting attorney. He told me to come and clean out my office Sunday night. I overslept, and that's why I'm here this early in the morning."

"How do we know that you're telling the truth? You could be here because Jack told you to meet him here," David retorted skeptically.

"No! If that was the case, I would have walked in here with him," Carl argued, desperation creeping into his voice.

As the scene unfolded, Carl's mind whirred back to a past conversation. A flashback struck him- Jack mentioning that it was too late to go to the bank and that he would do it first thing Monday morning. Realization dawned on Carl, the significance of what that meant- all of the money was now his, a staggering $40 million.

ᘏᗢ

"Do you think we should believe him?" Jerry asked, eyeing Carl with suspicion.

"I can give you all a good reason to believe me. Jack and I have some money saved up, and I will give you his entire share," Carl offered, trying to persuade them.

"How much is his share?" David inquired, intrigued by the prospect.

"$20 million, and you all can split it three ways. Now that Jack is dead, I'm the one who has control of the money," Carl explained.

Jerry paused, considering the offer. "If Jack had $20 million, that means so do you. I think it should be all or nothing. Either we split $40 million three ways, and you walk out of here with your life, or we get nothing, and I will personally put you in this microwave right now. What do you think, Otis and David?"

"We agree with you," Otis and David replied in unison, nodding firmly.

"Now the choice is yours, Carl. Is it a deal?" Jerry pressed.

Carl, visibly scared, relented. "Okay, it's a deal. I guess it wasn't meant for me to have because Jack was going to keep my share too. As soon as the banks open in the morning, I'll transfer the money into your accounts. You all will sign for it, and then I can walk away with my life, right? Deal?"

David, Otis, and Jerry nodded in agreement.

"David! Handcuff Carl to the rail on the stage steps to make sure he doesn't go anywhere, but first dismiss the prisoners," Otis instructed.

David proceeded to handle the task, ensuring that Carl wouldn't escape. With the prisoners dismissed and Carl restrained, the three men stood together, ready to face the consequences of their actions and the new future that awaited them.

"Okay," David responded, grabbing the microphone to address the prisoners. "Alright, everybody, the show is over. Go back to your cells."

As the prisoners began to depart, David waited until the room was nearly empty before handcuffing Carl to the rail. A few prisoners caught sight of what was happening, making eye contact with Carl as they left the room.

"David and Jerry, please come here for a minute," Otis called. The two men approached, curious.

"What is it?" David asked.

"Whose idea was it to bring the prisoners in here to watch this?" Otis inquired, looking at them both.

"It was my idea," Jerry admitted.

"Why?" Otis wanted to know.

"I felt like because of all that they'd been through, they should be a part of this," Jerry explained.

"I sure hope this doesn't backfire," Otis muttered, concern flickering in his eyes.

"They're all prisoners. If any of them talk, who's going to believe them? They have no credibility, and it's our word against theirs," David reasoned.

"I sure hope that you're right," Otis echoed, clearly still anxious about the potential consequences.

Later that day, David, Jerry, and Otis sat in David's office, still reveling in their newfound wealth.

"It sure is nice to have $13 million, $333 thousand, and $333 dollars and thirty-three cents. HA! HA!" David laughed.

"You know it," Otis agreed, grinning.

"Carl couldn't wait to get away from us. Did you see how fast he jumped in that cab? HA! HA!" Jerry joined in the laughter.

Their jovial conversation was interrupted by a knock on the door.

"Come on in," David called.

To their shock, the door opened to reveal Carl.

"What are you doing here, Carl?" Otis asked, stunned.

"I'm here doing my job as the prosecuting attorney," Carl stated plainly.

"I thought you said that Jack fired you," Jerry pointed out, puzzled.

"He did, but just like he didn't get a chance to go to the bank, he also didn't get a chance to make my termination official. So, I'm still the prosecuting attorney, and you all are under arrest for the murder of Governor Warden Jack Blake!" Carl announced.

"You can't prove it. You didn't see us do it!" David protested.

"No, I didn't, but they did," Carl retorted, motioning for the prisoners who'd made eye contact with him earlier to come in. Their faces showed shock at the sight of the prisoners.

"Who is going to believe them? They're just prisoners," Jerry scoffed, trying to downplay the situation.

"Everybody, when I back them up. They also saw David handcuff me to the rail. You guys will be charged with kidnapping and holding for ransom. I have the bank statements to prove that I signed over $40 million to all three of you. Plus, Otis showed me the remains of Jack and admitted to me that you all killed him. I think that will be enough to get you all convicted," Carl explained confidently, delivering a reality check that left the room in stunned silence.

David, Otis and Jerry are scared and look very nervous

"Why? Why are you doing this? You knew that Jack had to be stopped. After all, he tried to fire you," Otis protested, visibly upset.

"Being fired is one thing, but do you think that I'm going to hand over $40 million to three guys that were going to kill me? You're crazy! But that's what money does to people," Carl reasoned, his voice stern.

"Jack had a problem, true enough, but his real troubles began when he started making too much money. He became too damn greedy! Instead of being satisfied with what he had, it was like the more he would get, the more he would want until it ruined him, and now he ended up with nothing, not even his life. You all could have had $6.5 million each if you all had taken the offer. But just like Jack, the more you were going to get, the more you wanted! You all are so greedy; therefore, you will end up with nothing, not even your life. And just because Jack is gone doesn't mean that the microwave won't live on. I'm going to put you all in it, just like you all put Jack in it!"

"I knew we should've killed him," Jerry snapped, anger flaring in his eyes. He opened a cabinet and reached for a rifle.

"I wouldn't do that if I were you. Do you think that I was dumb enough to come here by myself?" Carl warned, looking at Jerry.

"Who's going to help you, the prisoners? I'll kill them too," Jerry threatened, his hand gripping the rifle tighter.

"No! Not them," Carl retorted, raising his voice slightly."James!"

At Carl's call, James rushed in with twelve state troopers, their guns aimed at Jerry, Otis, and David.

"Place these men under arrest and get them out of here," Carl instructed the troopers, who quickly complied and apprehended the three men.

"You will be free men once they're convicted. Thank you all for being willing to testify," Carl said, addressing the prisoners, who thanked him profusely.

After the prisoners had left, Carl sat down behind David's desk and picked up the phone. After a brief exchange, he hung up, elation washing over him.

With a triumphant yell of "YEAH!!!" he threw his hands into the air, finally able to relax now that justice had been served.

THE END

Printed in the USA
CPSIA information can be obtained
at www.ICGtesting.com
LVHW051554190424
777903LV00002B/227